The Back Stories of History featuring South Community

Priscilla T Graham

ISBN: 978-1-953824-19-6

Printed in the United States of America

In the making of this book, every attempt has been made to verify names, facts, and figures. Sources: Texas Historical Association, National Register for Historic Places, Texas Historical Commission Markers, findagrave.com, ancestry.com, Church Cornerstones, and Dedication Markers

Photos from the Graham Collection

Written by Priscilla T Graham
priscillatgraham.com@gmail.com

Cover Design and layout by Priscilla T Graham

Dedicated to the men and women of the South Community!

Black History is American History.

Content

Preface 5
Virginia Point 7
The Birth of Texas City and the Migration of Freedmen 11
Building a Community Work, Family, and Daily Life 15
The Spiritual Corridor: First Avenue South 20
The Churches That Built the Community 24
Galilee Methodist Church 25
First Baptist Church 27
Barbour's Chapel Baptist Church 30
A Shared Spiritual Foundation 34
Transition: When the City Caught Up 35
Education and the Rise of Booker T. Washington School 37
Wings and Boots: The Army and Aviation 48
The Great Depression 51
World War II and the Transformation of Texas City 54
The Texas City Disaster of 1947 57
Postwar Growth, Civil Rights, and Community Evolution 62
Legacy, Memory, and the Diaspora of the South Community 66
Erasure, Green Space, and the Fight for Memory 70
Legacy Preservation and Institutional Memory 75
The South Community Lives On
Continuity, Responsibility, and the Present Moment 78
Displacement 81
From Narrative to Record 83
African American Historical Cultural Park 85
References 141
About the Author 144

Preface

For much of the twentieth century, the South Community occupied a ten-block district formally bounded by Texas Avenue to the north, 10th Street to the west, Fourth Avenue to the south, and 5th Street to the east. While the neighborhood is sometimes remembered as nine blocks in oral tradition, municipal mapping and city documentation define the area as a ten-block district. This ten-block footprint reflects the city-recognized boundaries within which Black families built homes, churches, schools, businesses, and institutions that sustained community life for generations.

It was a tightly knit neighborhood built by Black American families navigating segregation, industrial labor, disaster, and exclusion with intention, faith, and collective care. Its churches, schools, businesses, and homes formed an intergenerational world shaped by proximity, shared responsibility, and collective survival. As Texas City's physical landscape changed, much of that history was pushed to the margins of public record.

This book documents what existed.

The South Community was not a peripheral settlement or a temporary enclave. It was deliberately built by families shaped by post-emancipation migration and constrained by racial boundaries that dictated where Black residents could live, work, and worship. Its people labored in refineries, rail yards, docks, and military supply chains that powered the city's growth, often under dangerous conditions. At the same time, they built churches along First Avenue South, created educational spaces for their children, and sustained mutual aid networks that carried families through depression, war, hurricane, and industrial catastrophe.

Drawing from oral histories, church records, municipal documents, and archival sources, this book treats lived experience as historical evidence central to understanding how the community functioned and why it endured. It traces not only construction and survival, but also the forces that reshaped the neighborhood over time.

Displacement did not arrive as a single decision or dramatic moment. It unfolded gradually through zoning changes, industrial expansion, infrastructure withdrawal, and the reclassification of lived neighborhoods as buffers and green space. Homes and churches disappeared from the landscape, but the community did not. Families carried memory, values, and responsibility beyond the original footprint. What follows is a history of construction, endurance, and transformation. The South Community did not vanish. It evolved from a neighborhood into a lineage, from lived space into remembered ground, and this book stands as a record of that history.

Virginia Point

Access to Galveston and the South Community

The construction of a wagon bridge from Virginia Point to Galveston Island in 1893 marked a significant shift in how people, goods, and labor moved along the Galveston Bay corridor. By providing a direct route for transporting farm produce from the Settlement and other mainland farms into Galveston's markets, the bridge strengthened Virginia Point's role as a gateway between rural Galveston County and the island's port economy. This connection reshaped patterns of commerce and mobility that long predated Texas City's industrial rise and formed part of the broader geographic landscape into which the South Community would later emerge.

For Black American families navigating the post-emancipation South, access corridors like Virginia Point held particular importance. These routes linked agricultural labor, dock work, and market activity, shaping how Black workers moved across space within a segregated society.

Long before Texas City was fully established as an industrial hub, Black labor already flowed through these pathways, hauling crops, working docks, and sustaining the economies that connected mainland farms to Galveston's port. The bridge did not create the South Community, but it formed part of the transportation and economic network that made migration, work, and settlement along Galveston Bay possible.

When Texas City began to industrialize in the early twentieth century, these earlier routes of movement and labor helped explain why Black families were already familiar with the region and prepared to seize new opportunities. The South Community developed within this larger geography of access, close to rail lines, port facilities, and industrial employment, rather than in isolation. Its emergence reflected continuity as much as change, grounded in patterns of labor and mobility that had been in motion for decades.

The annexation of Virginia Point by Texas City on March 28, 1952, occurred much later, after the South Community had already been established for generations and had endured the Depression, World War II, and the Texas City Disaster of 1947.

This annexation reflected mid-century municipal expansion and the consolidation of land tied to transportation, industry, and strategic access points. Although Virginia Point was never part of the original ten-block South Community, its incorporation into Texas City illustrates how municipal boundaries continued to shift long after Black residents had built their neighborhood, churches, and institutions.

In this way, Virginia Point frames the South Community's story rather than defining it. The bridge represents early regional connectivity that shaped labor and migration patterns along Galveston Bay. At the same time, the 1952 annexation underscores how the city expanded outward even as the historic Black neighborhood faced increasing pressure, displacement, and eventual erasure.

Together, these developments reveal a recurring truth in the South Community's history: Black families built enduring places within a landscape that was continually reshaped by transportation, industry, and city planning decisions made beyond their control.

The Birth of Texas City and the Migration of Freedmen

The dawn of the twentieth century marked a pivotal moment for the region surrounding Galveston Bay. In 1893, a group of Midwestern investors operating as the Texas City Improvement Company first imagined an industrial port along the bay's western shoreline. Their early efforts faltered, but the vision endured. By 1898, the United States government selected the site for a deep-water port and military encampment, accelerating development and anchoring the area's strategic importance. Within a few years, what had once been open coastal land began to take shape as a planned industrial city.

By 1905, Texas City was formally platted as a new municipality just a few miles east of the original Settlement. Its location was deliberate. Positioned along the shoreline and connected by rail, the city was designed to become a major hub for shipping, refining, and industrial production. The establishment of the port marked more than local growth; it signaled a transformation in the economic geography of

Southeast Texas, drawing labor, capital, and infrastructure into a rapidly changing landscape.

That transformation accelerated with the discovery of oil at Spindletop in 1901. The oil boom reshaped the Gulf Coast almost overnight, and Texas City stood at the center of that expansion. The Texas City Refining Company, among the earliest refineries on the coast, rose along the waterfront in the first decade of the twentieth century. Its presence drew additional investment, expanded port operations, and created a sustained demand for labor. Rail lines multiplied. Tank farms, warehouses, and industrial facilities spread across the shoreline, forming an industrial corridor that promised steady wages at a time when rural life offered little beyond agricultural labor and seasonal uncertainty.

The families who would later build the South Community were living in the generations immediately following emancipation. Freedom had been declared in Texas in 1865, but what followed was not security or equality. Black Texans entered a post-emancipation landscape defined by restricted land access, racial violence, and economic dependency, conditions that required constant negotiation and self-determination. It was within this environment that patterns of migration, labor, and settlement along Galveston Bay began to take shape, laying the groundwork for the community that would emerge in Texas City.

For Black American families navigating the decades after emancipation, Texas City represented possibility. Across Texas and Louisiana, Freedmen and their descendants faced the grinding realities of sharecropping, tenant farming, racial violence, and economic instability. Industrial work, though dangerous and discriminatory, offered wages paid in cash and the chance to step outside the cycles that had bound Black labor to the land since Reconstruction. Families began leaving farms, piney woods, and rural communities in search of opportunity.

Others arrived from Galveston itself. The devastation of the 1900 Storm displaced thousands, including many Black families who were forced to seek new beginnings on the mainland. Texas City, still young and expanding, became one of the places where those displaced families rebuilt their lives. They came carrying skills honed in agriculture, domestic work, dock labor, and trades. They also brought with them faith traditions, kinship networks, and a determination to build something lasting in a world that rarely offered security.

By 1911, Texas City had grown enough to hold its first city elections and adopt a mayor-commissioner form of government. As the city formalized its civic identity, Black American families were already shaping their own. They settled in a compact residential district south of the expanding industrial corridor, a neighborhood that would become the heart of Black Texas City.

This district, consistently identified in oral histories, city maps, and early property records, formed the foundation of what came to be known as the South Community. Within this defined footprint, Freedmen and their descendants began building a world rooted in resilience, faith, and collective purpose. They did not arrive to empty land in an empty city. They arrived into segregation, into racial boundaries that dictated where they could live, work, and gather. What they built within those boundaries was intentional.

Families brought with them traditions of mutual aid and community building that had sustained them through enslavement, Reconstruction, and migration. In Texas City, those traditions took new shape. Homes were built and expanded. Gardens were planted. Small businesses opened. Churches and fraternal lodges emerged as centers of worship, education, and social life. These institutions were not gifts from the city; they were the result of collective effort in a segregated environment that offered little institutional support.

The South Community did not emerge by accident. It was created by families who sought safety, belonging, and opportunity in a city that relied on their labor while denying them equality. Men worked in refineries, rail yards, and on the docks, performing some of the most dangerous jobs in the industrial economy. Women anchored households, raised children, managed finances, and sustained the social networks that held the neighborhood together. Together, they built a place where dignity could exist, even when the world beyond its boundaries denied it.

This marks the beginning of that story: the rise of Texas City as an industrial power, the migration of Black families into its orbit, and the formation of a neighborhood that would become the spiritual, cultural, and historical center of Black life in the city. It is the story of people who arrived with little, recognized opportunity amid constraints, and laid the groundwork for a community that would endure for generations.

Building a Community

Work, Family, and Daily Life

As Texas City grew into an industrial hub in the early twentieth century, the South Community became far more than a place where Black American families lived. It became a world shaped by their own hands, defined by work, faith, kinship, and the daily discipline of survival. Located just south of the expanding industrial corridor, the neighborhood's position placed Black families within walking distance of the refineries, rail yards, and port facilities where many of them labored. This proximity shaped the rhythm of daily life and anchored the community's identity.

Families who arrived from rural Texas, Louisiana, and Galveston brought with them traditions of self-reliance and collective care. These traditions took root quickly. Within the historic footprint of the South Community, neighbors built a close-knit environment where every household contributed to the strength of the whole. Oral histories and early city maps consistently identify this compact district as the primary residential center for Black families during the first half of the twentieth century. Density was not accidental; it fostered protection, cooperation, and shared responsibility in a segregated city that offered little margin for error.

Work shaped nearly every aspect of life. Men labored long hours in refineries, rail yards, and on the docks, jobs that were physically demanding and often dangerous, yet among the few that provided steady wages. Their labor powered the city's growth while exposing them to constant risk. Women's work, equally essential, extended across households and the wider community. They managed homes, raised children, took in laundry, cooked for neighbors, worked in domestic service, and anchored the informal economies that kept families afloat.

Together, men's and women's labor sustained the neighborhood through both prosperity and hardship.

Entrepreneurship flourished early within the South Community. Black men and women opened grocery stores, cafés, service shops, and small businesses that served both their neighbors and the broader city. These enterprises were more than sources of income. They were assertions of independence in a segregated world that limited opportunity at every turn.

Business owners became community anchors, providing goods, services, and stability that helped families navigate the uncertainties of industrial labor and racial discrimination. In a city where Black residents were excluded from many public accommodations, these businesses affirmed self-sufficiency and dignity.

Daily life blended practicality with pride. Families tended gardens, raised chickens, and shared food with neighbors. Bartering and resource self-sufficiency were common, not solely because of scarcity, but because these practices were deeply rooted in cultural traditions of survival and mutual obligation. Children played in yards and along unpaved streets, watched over by adults who understood that every child belonged to the community as a whole. Elders passed down stories, values, and expectations that shaped behavior and reinforced a sense of belonging.

Respect for age, discipline, and responsibility was taught not only at home but also collectively.

Education occupied a central place in community life. Before Booker T. Washington School had a permanent building, children learned wherever space could be found, in church sanctuaries, lodge halls, and borrowed rooms that doubled as classrooms and meeting places. This pattern reflected a broader reality across segregated Texas, where Black communities often had to create educational spaces long before school districts provided formal facilities. Volunteer teachers, donated materials, and parents' insistence on discipline and achievement sustained these early efforts. Education was understood not simply as instruction, but as protection and possibility.

When the Texas City Independent School District finally established a dedicated school building in 1937, it became a symbol of progress and pride. Though modest, it offered permanence and stability. Families rallied around the school, reinforcing expectations of respect, effort, and excellence. Booker T. Washington School quickly became more than a place of instruction; it became a center of neighborhood life, shaping children who would carry the community's values forward.

Spiritual life was woven into the fabric of everyday living. The churches that lined and surrounded First Avenue South, Galilee Methodist Church, Barbour's Chapel Baptist Church, and the nearby First Baptist Church, structured the moral and social life of the neighborhood. Sundays were devoted to worship and fellowship, but the churches' influence extended far beyond Sunday mornings. Weekdays brought choir rehearsals, prayer meetings, youth programs, women's auxiliaries, and gatherings that strengthened bonds across families and generations.

These churches functioned as far more than places of worship. They served as civic institutions, social networks, and places of refuge. When a family struggled, the churches mobilized. When illness struck, help arrived. When hardship threatened to overwhelm, faith and community intervened. This collective vigilance created a sense of safety and belonging that stood in stark contrast to the segregation and surveillance that shaped life outside the neighborhood. Mutual aid was not an occasional gesture; it was a way of life.

The South Community operated on an unspoken understanding: no one was left to struggle alone. Extended families shared homes. Neighbors watched one another's children. Resources were pooled, news was exchanged, and responsibility was shared. These practices were not romantic ideals; they were practical strategies forged through generations of survival. They allowed families to endure low wages, dangerous work, and systemic exclusion without losing cohesion.

Through steady labor, shared responsibility, and unwavering faith, the families of the South Community built a neighborhood that was both resilient and vibrant. They created a place where dignity was defended, where children were nurtured, and where the values carried from earlier generations, perseverance, unity, and hope, were lived daily. The community's strength did not come from wealth or political power. It came from people who understood that survival required cooperation, and that belonging had to be built and protected.

This chapter captures the heartbeat of that world: the work that sustained it, the families who defined it, the businesses that anchored it, and the traditions that held it together. It reveals how ordinary routines, working, worshiping, learning, and caring for one another, became acts of quiet resistance and collective purpose within the South Community.

Texas City
First African - American Church Street
First Avenue South
February, 2000
We dedicate First Avenue South / Martin Luther King, Jr. Avenue to the memory of our many ancestors, families, friends and visitors who started their religious affiliations on First Avenue South at either Galilee Methodist Church, First Baptist Church or Barboure Chapel Baptist Church during the first quarter of this century (1900) in Texas City. The spiritual legacy of those who pastored, preached, fellowshipped or worshipped God on this street will never be forgotten.
*Galilee United Methodist Church
1913 Bishop A.G. Brooks / Rev. H.F. Hynson, 2000
*First Missionary Baptist Church
1914 Rev. Steve / Rev. F.M. Johnson, 2000
Barbours Chapel Baptist Church
1913 Rev. Barbour / Rev. H.A. Ratcliff, 2000
A tribute to
Martin Luther King, Jr.
January 15, 1929 - April 4, 1968
This avenue where our early African churches were constructed is named in the memory of a man of great moral presence who donated his life to the fight for full citizenship rights of the poor, disadvantaged and racially oppressed. He was the second of three children of the Rev. Michael and Mrs. Alberta Williams King of Atlanta, GA. He received a bachelor's degree in sociology (1948) from Moorehouse College, a bachelor's degree (1951) from Croscu Theological Seminary and a doctorate in philosophy (1955) from Boston University.
In 1954, King accepted his first pastorate - the Dexter Avenue Baptist Church in Montgomery, Alabama. He and his wife, Coretta Scott King, whom he had met and married (June 1953) at Boston University, had been living in Montgomery less than a year when Rosa Parks defied the ordinance concerning segregated seating on city buses (Dec 1955). King's successful bus boycott, with the help of Rev. Ralph Abernathy and Edward Nixon, catapulted him into national prominence as a leader of the Civil Rights movement.
King studied the life and teachings of Mahatma Gandhi and further developed the Indian leader's doctrine of Salyagraha (holding to the truth) on non-violent civil disobedience. In 1960, he accepted co-pastorship with his father at Ebenezer Baptist Church in Atlanta.
He worked on voter registration campaigns throughout the South and organized the massive March on Washington (August 28, 1963) where his brilliant "I Have a Dream" speech "subpoenaed the conscience of the nation before the judgement seat of morality." In January 1964, TIME magazine chose King "Man of the Year", the first black American so honored. The same year, he became the youngest recipient of the Nobel Peace Prize. He led the harrowing march from Selma to Montgomery in March 1965. In Washington, he spoke out against the Vietnam War, which took funds from the war on poverty. In the midst of assisting striking workers in Memphis, Tennessee, on April 4, 1968, King was felled by an assassin's bullet. The nation was deprived of a towering symbol of moral and social progress. In 1983, King's birthday was designated a national holiday.
Marker prepared by Commissioner Lynn Ray Ellison, District 3
and Mayor Charles T. Doyle.

The Spiritual Corridor: First Avenue South

Before the city paved it, widened it, or renamed it in honor of Dr. Martin Luther King Jr., First Avenue South was already sacred ground. Long before it appeared on official plats or signage, it held a deeper distinction: it was the first place in Texas City where Black families could gather without fear, worship without restriction, and build institutions that reflected their own dignity. The people who lived along this stretch of road understood its significance long before the city ever acknowledged it.

To understand why First Avenue South became holy ground, it is necessary to understand the world in which it emerged. At the turn of the twentieth century, Texas City was a place in constant motion. Railroads expanded. Refineries rose along the shoreline. The port grew busier by the year. Workers arrived from every direction, drawn by the promise of industrial employment. Black families came from Galveston after the devastation of the 1900 Storm, from Louisiana parishes, from East Texas pinewoods, and from rural communities where worship often took place in brush arbors or small praise houses built by hand. They carried more than belongings. They carried memory, faith, and the determination to build a life in a segregated city that offered little space for Black humanity.

Texas City offered opportunity, but it did not offer belonging. Jim Crow dictated where Black families could live, work, and worship. Public facilities were segregated. Social spaces were policed. In the city's early years, there were no established Black churches, no community centers, and no institutions created for Black American residents. The absence was not accidental; it reflected the racial order of the time. Faced with this reality, Black families did what they had always done. They built their own.

Within the area known as the Second Division—one of the earliest platted residential sections of Texas City—families formed a tightly knit neighborhood shaped by kinship, shared labor, and collective survival.

At the heart of this neighborhood stood First Avenue South, an unassuming street that would become the most important spiritual artery in the city. Between 1905 and 1913, three congregations emerged that defined the spiritual identity of Black Texas City: First Baptist Church (1905), Galilee Methodist Church (1913), and Barbour's Chapel Baptist Church (1913). These founding dates are preserved in church records, anniversary programs, and Texas Historical Commission documentation.

These churches were not built with wealth, political influence, or institutional support. They were built with donated lumber, hand-mixed concrete, and the labor of men and women who worked long hours in refineries, rail yards, domestic service, and on the docks. Construction often took place after exhausting shifts, on weekends, and through pooled resources. The buildings rose because the people believed that faith was not optional. It was essential.

For many families, these churches became their first spiritual homes in Texas City. Earliest memories of belonging were formed along First Avenue South—baptisms held in wooden pools or at the bay, weddings that united families, funerals that honored ancestors, revivals that filled the street with song and prayer, and Sunday School lessons that shaped identity and expectation. Youth programs nurtured leadership. Choirs cultivated discipline and pride. This was not simply a street with churches. It was a spiritual ecosystem where Black life could breathe, grow, and endure.

During segregation, space was never neutral. Every street carried a message: you belong here, or you do not. First Avenue South answered that question clearly for Black families. Here, they belonged. The churches created a protected zone where families could gather without fear of intrusion or harassment. On Sunday mornings, the avenue filled with people dressed in their best, greeting neighbors, exchanging news, and checking on the sick and the elderly. On weeknights, the glow of church windows spilled onto the street during choir rehearsals, prayer meetings, and youth activities.

This constant movement created a form of collective protection. If a child walked home alone, someone knew their name. If a family struggled, the churches mobilized. If danger approached, it rarely went unnoticed. In a city that demanded Black silence, these churches taught Black children to speak. In a world that denied Black humanity, they affirmed it. In a society that sought to confine Black life, they expanded it.

Generations later, when the community dedicated the street, the words chosen reflected what residents had always known to be true:

We dedicate First Avenue South / Martin Luther King Jr. Avenue to the memory of our many ancestors, families, friends, and visitors who started their religious affiliations on First Avenue South...

This dedication was not symbolic language layered onto an ordinary place. It was a recognition of lived truth. First Avenue South was not merely geography. It was lineage. It was testimony. It was the first spiritual home of Black Texas City.

Along this corridor, faith took root. Community was forged. Generations began their walk with God. The churches that rose there shaped not only worship practices, but the moral, cultural, and social foundations of the South Community. They taught children who they were. They reminded adults of what they were building. And they sustained a people navigating a world that offered little protection beyond what they created for themselves.

First Avenue South remains sacred ground—not because the city eventually named it so, but because Black families consecrated it through worship, labor, sacrifice, and faith long before recognition ever came.

The Churches That Built the Community

The spiritual life of the South Community did not emerge all at once. It grew congregation by congregation, family by family, through the labor of people who understood that faith was both refuge and foundation.

The churches that rose along and around First Avenue South—Galilee Methodist Church, First Baptist Church, and Barbour's Chapel Baptist Church—became the institutions that shaped the identity, rhythm, and resilience of Black Texas City.

These churches were not established through wealth or political power. They were built with donated lumber, hand-mixed concrete, and the determination of men and women who worked long hours in refineries, rail yards, domestic service, and the port. Construction happened after exhausting shifts, on weekends, and through pooled resources. Each structure stood as evidence of collective sacrifice and shared belief. The buildings mattered, but what mattered more was what happened inside them.

From their earliest days, these churches functioned as far more than places of worship. They were gathering spaces, classrooms, meeting halls, and centers of protection. They offered structure in a city where Black families were denied access to most public institutions. Through sermons, Sunday School lessons, women's auxiliaries, youth programs, and fellowship gatherings, the churches shaped moral life, reinforced discipline, and cultivated leadership. They became the backbone of the South Community's social order.

Galilee Methodist Church

The first organized spiritual gathering place for Black families in the Second Division

Galilee Methodist Church stands among the earliest organized expressions of Black religious life in Texas City. Formally founded in January 1913, it holds significance as one of the first places where Black families could gather consistently for worship and fellowship. The congregation initially met in a tin building on 6th Street, within walking distance of First Avenue South, making it accessible to families settling in the Second Division. This early location is confirmed in church records and oral histories.

For many families arriving from Galveston, Louisiana, and rural Texas, Galilee was the first church they joined in their new city. It offered stability during a period marked by segregation, industrial labor demands, and the uncertainties of migration. Even before a permanent building was constructed prior to 1917, Galilee served as a spiritual anchor. Sunday School, women's ministries, youth programs, and community gatherings shaped daily life and reinforced the values that sustained families navigating an often-hostile world.

Galilee's story is inseparable from the story of First Avenue South. Its early presence helped establish the spiritual corridor that would become the birthplace of Black worship in Texas City. The church provided continuity during years of rapid change and laid the groundwork for the broader religious ecosystem that followed.

First Baptist Church

An early Baptist presence whose proximity shaped the emerging Black religious district

First Baptist Church, founded on March 16, 1905, predates the formal establishment of the Black congregations that would later define First Avenue South. Located on 4th Avenue North near Danforth School, it stood close enough to the Second Division that Black families frequently attended programs, revivals, funerals, and community gatherings there before their own churches were fully established.

While First Baptist was not exclusively Black American, its early presence contributed to the religious landscape in which Black congregations emerged. For many families, it served as their first point of worship in Texas City. These early experiences shaped expectations of church life and community responsibility that would later be carried into Galilee and Barbour's Chapel.

In 1932, First Baptist launched a Mexican Mission, reflecting a broader vision of outreach that influenced the surrounding neighborhoods.

In community memory, First Baptist remains part of the South Community's story because it represents the transitional space between exclusion and self-determination—an early site of worship before Black families were able to fully build institutions of their own.

ST
M.L.KING
STOP

Barbour's Chapel Baptist Church

The heart of First Avenue South and the church that defined the community's spiritual identity

Barbour's Chapel Baptist Church, founded in October 1913 by Reverend Russel C. Barbour, became the congregation most deeply intertwined with the identity of First Avenue South. Located at 801 First Avenue South, the church stood at the center of the Black neighborhood—physically, spiritually, and culturally. Its location is documented in city directories, church records, and Texas Historical Commission site files.

For generations, Barbour's Chapel served as the first church home for Black families in Texas City. It was where children were baptized, choirs were formed, and youth learned leadership and discipline.

Weddings, funerals, revivals, and anniversaries anchored family life to the church calendar. Ministries, usher boards, missionary societies, and educational programs shaped the social fabric of the avenue and extended care far beyond the sanctuary walls.

After the Texas City Disaster of 1947, Barbour's Chapel became a refuge for Black families who were often excluded from white relief centers. The church provided food, clothing, medical assistance, and shelter, earning its reputation as the "little church with a big heart." Survivor accounts and local histories consistently document its role during this period, marking it as a cornerstone of communal survival during one of the city's darkest moments.

In 1952, Barbour's Chapel established the first Black American church-based college fund in Galveston County, extending its mission beyond spiritual life into educational opportunity. This initiative reflected a long-standing belief within the South Community that faith and advancement were inseparable.

The original building, known as *The Castle*, its cornerstone and bell were preserved and now rest in the Black American Cultural Park. These artifacts stand as tangible reminders of the church's enduring presence and its central role in shaping generations of Black Texans.

Barbour's Chapel remains the clearest embodiment of why First Avenue South is sacred ground.

From Whence We Came
Frederick Douglass
Booker T. Washington
Mary Mcleod Bethume
W.E.B. Du Bois
Harriet Tubman
Sojourner Truth
George Washington Carver
Nat Turner
Paul Lawrence Dunbar
Phyllis Wheatley
Langston Hughes
Crisper Attucks
HISTORICAL
TEXAS
CITY
MARKER
Medgar Evers
Rosa Parks
Jackie Robinson
Thurgood Marshall
Adam Clayton Powell
Dr. Martin Luther King, Jr.
Muhammad Ali
Al Sharpton
Jessie Jackson
President Barack Obama
(44th U.S. President)
Michelle Obama
AFRICAN AMERICAN HISTORICAL MARKER!
Texas City, Texas
This marker is dedicated in respect and honor for the original African American community in Texas City, Texas, incorporated in 1911. When African Americans first came to Texas City as wards, there was no encouragement for them to settle here. The need for laborers on the docks, waterfronts, construction of sugar refineries and other major industries made them necessary. We honor our parents, teachers, schools, principals, churches, pastors, ministers, friends and neighbors, as well as others who came here from cotton gin towns, watermelon patch towns, saw-mill towns, and from corn, cane, rice and tobacco fields, all over the south hoping for a better life in segregated towns. From Texas Avenue on the North, 10th Street on the West, Bay Street on the East and Fourth Avenue on the South, this sacred community of nine square blocks is our "Mecca". This marker represents all of those individuals and families who settled, worked, worshipped and raised families here.
YOU WILL NEVER BE FORGOTTEN!
OUR FAMILIES AND FRIENDS THAT LIVED HERE
ORIGINAL SOUTHSIDE COMMUNITY HISTORICAL PROJECT PHASE I
Lynn Ray Ellison - President - Clarence Caldwell - Vice President - Bobbie Alford Garrett - Treasurer
Doris Conley / Mary Johnson - Secretaries - Special Project: All The B.T.W. Ex's
SUMMER 2015

A Shared Spiritual Foundation

When the community later dedicated First Avenue South, they were not honoring three separate churches in isolation. They were honoring a shared spiritual birthplace, the place where Black Texas City learned to worship, organize, and endure.

They honored:

- the families who joined their first church there
- the children who learned their first prayers there
- the elders who built institutions from nothing
- the pastors who led through segregation, disaster, and change
- the generations who found belonging along the avenue

First Avenue South is where the community's spiritual identity began. It is where faith took root and where collective strength was forged. The churches that built the South Community did more than meet religious needs. They sustained a people, shaped a culture, and preserved dignity in a world that offered little protection beyond what the community created for itself.

Transition: When the City Caught Up

By the middle of the twentieth century, the South Community was no longer a marginal neighborhood on the edge of Texas City. It was established, rooted, and intergenerational. Black families had built churches, schools, businesses, and social networks that endured economic depression, war, and disaster. Their presence was neither temporary nor accidental. It was the result of decades of labor, faith, and intentional place-making within a segregated city that depended on their work while limiting their rights.

Yet the very forces that made the South Community possible, industry, transportation, and municipal growth, would also place it at increasing risk. As Texas City expanded, land values shifted, infrastructure projects multiplied, and city planning decisions began to reshape the physical landscape with little regard for the people who had built lives there. What had once been peripheral became contested. What had been ignored became targeted.

The story that follows is not one of sudden disappearance, but of pressure applied over time. It is the story of how a stable Black neighborhood was gradually destabilized through policy, planning, and expansion, often framed as progress, efficiency, or modernization. It is also the story of how residents resisted erasure through memory, institution building, and the preservation of identity long after physical space was lost.

To understand what was taken, it is first necessary to understand what existed. Only then can the full weight of what followed be measured.

Education and the Rise of Booker T. Washington School

Before Texas City built a school for Black children, education in the South Community was a grassroots act of determination. Families who had survived enslavement, Reconstruction, and migration understood that literacy was not simply a skill. It was protection. It was advancement. It was a declaration of dignity in a society that worked actively to deny it. In the early years, children learned wherever space could be found—inside churches, lodge halls, and borrowed rooms that doubled as sanctuaries, meeting places, and centers of community life.

These makeshift classrooms were held together by volunteer teachers, donated books, and parents who insisted that their children would rise higher than the world expected. Lessons were taught around worship schedules and work shifts. Children learned to read, write, and recite under conditions that required discipline and patience. This model of education reflected a broader reality across segregated Texas, where

Black communities often had to create their own schools long before districts provided formal facilities.

For years, the South Community carried its educational responsibilities alone. Families pooled resources. Churches opened their doors. Elders reinforced expectations of respect and achievement. Education was treated as a collective obligation, not an individual pursuit. Every child's success mattered because it reflected the strength of the entire community.

That determination carried the neighborhood until 1937, when the Texas City Independent School District purchased property and moved a one-story wooden building onto the site that would become Booker T. Washington School. The structure was modest but permanent. For the first time, Black children in Texas City had a schoolhouse that belonged to them, one not borrowed, not temporary, and not subject to displacement by weather or worship schedules. School district records confirm that this building was among the earliest dedicated educational structures for Black American students in the city.

Instruction initially extended only through Grade 7. For years, students who wished to continue their education had to travel to Galveston's

Central High School, the first Black high school in Texas, established in 1885. The journey demanded sacrifice. Earlier generations crossed the bay by ferry. Later, students faced long commutes and transportation costs that strained already tight household budgets. Families made it work because they believed education was worth every mile.

Even with limited grades, Booker T. Washington School quickly became a cornerstone of the South Community. It was a place where children were nurtured, disciplined, and prepared for a world that demanded twice the effort for half the recognition. Teachers were not merely instructors; they were mentors, disciplinarians, and community figures. Parents reinforced school expectations at home, understanding that education was one of the few tools their children could carry into a segregated future.

As the community grew, so did the school. In 1946–47, a brick schoolhouse was constructed to house grades one through ten. The new building represented more than expansion. It stood as a testament to years of advocacy by Black families who had long pushed for better facilities and broader opportunity. The brick structure offered safety, permanence, and pride, qualities that radiated throughout the neighborhood. In 1953, a high school building was added, allowing students to complete their secondary education locally for the first time. No longer would children have to leave their community to finish school. The South Community had built its own educational pathway.

Leadership played a defining role in the school's development. Professor George Burr Sanders, the first principal of Booker T. Washington School, established a culture rooted in discipline, respect, and academic expectation. His leadership set a standard that shaped the school's early years and reinforced the belief that Black children deserved excellence, regardless of the limitations imposed upon them.

That legacy was carried forward by Calvin Vincent, who served as principal for twenty-four years. Under his guidance, the school became more than a place of instruction. It became a center of community life. Vincent's leadership spanned decades of social change, and his influence reached far beyond the classroom. Oral histories consistently remember both Sanders and Vincent as educators who demanded excellence, modeled integrity, and understood their responsibility not only to students, but to families and the wider community.

The impact of their leadership was so profound that the community later honored them through the creation of the Sanders/Vincent Community Center. Originally located south of Texas Avenue on the historic site of Booker T. Washington School, the center symbolized continuity between education, leadership, and community identity. When the modern facility opened in 2010 at 501 4th Avenue North, it carried forward the same mission: to provide a space for learning, gathering, and cultural celebration rooted in the values that shaped the South Community. Today, it stands as one of the few physical reminders of the neighborhood's educational legacy.

Throughout its history, Booker T. Washington School was more than a school. It was a sanctuary of possibility. It was where children learned to read, write, and imagine futures beyond the boundaries imposed upon them. It was where teachers became elders, principals became community leaders, and education became a collective act of resistance against the constraints of segregation.

The legacy of Booker T. Washington School lives on in the stories of those who walked its halls, in the families who fought for its existence, and in the institutions that continue to honor its spirit. It stands as a testament to the South Community's belief that education was not a privilege to be granted, but a birthright to be claimed—and defended—by every generation.

WASHINGTON
GYMNASIUM

1947
WASHINGTON GYMNASIUM

BOOKER T. WASHINGTON
1981 REUNION OF CLASSES
PRINCIPAL CALVIN VINCENT

Wings and Boots: The Army and Aviation

In 1913, Texas City became the stage for a remarkable convergence of military innovation and community transformation. That year, the United States Army deployed both the Second Division and the First Provisional Aero Squadron to the Gulf Coast in response to escalating tensions along the border during the Mexican Revolution. The Aero Squadron, established on March 5, 1913, was the Army's first aviation unit. Trained by the Wright Brothers themselves, it is now recognized as the direct ancestor of the United States Air Force. Their arrival placed Texas City at the center of a national military experiment, earning it recognition as the birthplace of military aviation.

The encampment was massive. More than 14,000 troops and 3,000 animals filled the city, joined by the unfamiliar sound of early aircraft engines rising above open fields. Temporary barracks, supply depots, and training grounds spread across the landscape. For Texas City, still a young industrial town, the presence of the Army transformed daily life almost overnight.

For the South Community compact neighborhood, where Black families had already begun building homes, churches, and businesses, the arrival of the military brought unprecedented opportunity. The Army required constant supplies and services: crops, hay, food preparation, laundry, hauling, and maintenance. Black residents stepped into these roles quickly, drawing on skills rooted in agricultural labor, domestic work, and entrepreneurship. For many families, this period marked one of the first times industrial and military demand translated into steady income and economic momentum.

Prosperity rippled through the neighborhood. Families pooled resources, expanded homes, and invested in their community. Churches along First Avenue South—Galilee Methodist, Barbour's Chapel, and the nearby First Baptist—became hubs not only of spiritual life but also of social coordination and mutual support. The economic activity generated by the encampment reinforced long-standing traditions of collective care, allowing families to stabilize their footing in a segregated city that otherwise offered few economic protections.

This period of growth, however, was fragile. In 1915, a powerful hurricane struck Texas City, devastating the Army encampment and forcing both the Second Division and the Aero Squadron to relocate inland to San Antonio. The departure was swift. With it went the military contracts, the steady flow of income, and the economic engine that had briefly transformed the city's fortunes.

For the South Community, the loss was immediate and deeply felt. Families who had come to rely on the work and wages provided by the encampment faced renewed uncertainty. Yet the response was neither collapse nor retreat. As they had done before, residents leaned on one another. Bartering expanded. Gardens were replanted. Extended families shared housing and resources. The same practices that had sustained Black communities through enslavement, Reconstruction, and migration once again became lifelines.

The story of the Army encampment and the birth of military aviation in Texas City is often told as a chapter of national significance. But for the South Community, it was also a lesson in impermanence and resilience. For a brief moment, the boots of thousands of soldiers and the wings of early aircraft brought prosperity and possibility. When the storm swept it away, the community endured, drawing on unity, faith, and collective responsibility to survive the sudden loss.

The legacy of this moment remains woven into the fabric of Texas City's history. It reminds us that even fleeting opportunities can leave lasting marks, and that the South Community's strength did not depend on the duration of prosperity, but on the depth of its resilience. Long after the planes departed and the camps disappeared, the values that sustained the neighborhood remained firmly grounded along First Avenue South.

The Great Depression

When the Great Depression swept across the United States between 1929 and 1939, it brought the nation to its knees. Banks failed. Factories closed. Unemployment soared to levels never before seen. Breadlines stretched for blocks. Families lost farms, homes, and savings. Entire regions collapsed under the weight of economic despair. For many Americans, survival itself became uncertain.

Yet within Texas City's South Community—the compact neighborhood anchored by First Avenue South—the Depression unfolded differently. The crisis did not bypass the community, but its impact was shaped by the unique industrial landscape of Texas City and the traditions of resilience already embedded in the lives of the families who lived there.

Texas City's economic backbone—the petroleum industry, the port, the rail lines, and the growing chemical plants—did not shut down during the Depression. These industries were considered essential. Oil still needed refining. Ships still needed loading. Rail lines still needed maintenance. Facilities tied to the Texas City Terminal Railway, the Texas City Refining Company, and the expanding industrial corridor continued operating throughout the 1930s. As a result, many Black men in the South Community remained employed even as millions across the country lost their jobs.

The work was demanding and often dangerous. Long hours, hazardous conditions, and racial discrimination were constants. Wages were low, and advancement was limited. Yet steady employment, however imperfect, provided a measure of stability that insulated the neighborhood from the total economic collapse experienced elsewhere. Oral histories from Texas City confirm that while hardship was real, the presence of industrial labor created a buffer that many rural and agricultural communities lacked.

This stability did not eliminate struggle. Families still faced overcrowded housing, limited access to public services, and the daily pressures of making ends meet. But starvation, mass displacement, and wholesale collapse were largely avoided. The South Community endured not because conditions were easy, but because families knew how to stretch what they had and how to survive together.

Long before the Depression arrived, residents had relied on practices passed down through generations. Gardening, bartering, food sharing, and pooled resources were not emergency measures invented in crisis; they were inherited traditions rooted in survival. When wages tightened and costs rose, the community expanded what it already knew how to do. Gardens grew more important. Extended families moved under one roof. Neighbors exchanged labor, food, and support without keeping score.

No one was allowed to fall alone.

The churches along First Avenue South—Galilee Methodist, Barbour's Chapel, and the nearby First Baptist—became even more vital during these years. They organized food baskets, clothing drives, and emergency collections. Fellowship halls served as places where families could share news, seek help, and find reassurance. In a period when federal relief programs were segregated, underfunded, or inaccessible to Black families, the churches functioned as the community's most reliable safety net.

Spiritual life offered stability when economic certainty disappeared. Sunday services provided encouragement and perspective. Prayer meetings, women's circles, and youth programs continued, reinforcing the sense that the community would endure even when the broader world seemed to unravel. Faith did not erase hardship, but it gave meaning and structure to survival.

Despite the strain of the 1930s, the South Community did not stagnate. In quiet ways, some families made progress. Homes were repaired or expanded. Land was purchased when possible. Church membership grew. Children continued attending school, carrying with them the discipline and expectations reinforced by both families and educators. The neighborhood's identity deepened as residents planted roots that would carry them through the next decade.

The Great Depression revealed what the South Community had already built. Its strength did not come from wealth, political power, or institutional support. It came from steady labor, shared responsibility, and the unwavering presence of the institutions that anchored daily life along First Avenue South.

The Depression did not break the South Community.
It tested it.
And the community endured.

As the nation struggled to regain its footing, the South Community emerged from the 1930s intact weathered but grounded in the same values that had sustained it from the beginning. Those values would soon be tested again, as global conflict reshaped Texas City and pulled the community into the demands of a world at war.

World War II and the Transformation of Texas City

As the 1930s drew to a close, the South Community had weathered the worst economic crisis in modern American history with a steadiness that set it apart from much of the nation. The Great Depression had tested families, churches, and institutions, but the combination of industrial labor, mutual aid, and spiritual grounding had carried the neighborhood through. Even as the economy slowly recovered, however, forces far beyond Texas City were already reshaping the future. The rumblings of war in Europe and Asia signaled another global shift—one that would soon reach the Gulf Coast.

When World War II erupted in 1939, and when the United States entered the conflict in 1941, Texas City was transformed almost overnight. The same industries that had sustained the city during the Depression became essential to the national war effort. Refineries increased production. The port expanded operations. Rail lines moved fuel, equipment, and materials critical to military logistics. Facilities tied to the Texas City Terminal Railway, Pan American Refinery, Republic Oil Refining Company, and the growing petrochemical corridor shifted into wartime production, binding the city directly to the demands of a world at war.

For the South Community, the war years brought both opportunity and strain. Black men who had held steady jobs throughout the 1930s now found their labor indispensable. Long shifts became the norm. Hazardous conditions intensified. The pressure to produce never eased. These jobs were grueling and often dangerous, but they offered wages that provided a rare measure of financial stability in earlier decades. Oral histories confirm that wartime employment allowed some families to purchase land, repair homes, and support relatives migrating from rural areas in search of work.

At the same time, the war pulled sons, brothers, and husbands into military service. Black American soldiers enlisted and were drafted into segregated units across the Army, Navy, and later the Women's Army Corps. They served with courage abroad while facing discrimination at home. Families in the South Community watched loved ones leave for training camps and distant battlefields, carrying both pride and fear. Letters from soldiers became lifelines—read aloud in living rooms and church gatherings, folded carefully, and saved as proof of survival.

Women's roles expanded dramatically during the war years. With so many men deployed or working extended shifts, women carried the weight of households, raised children, and sustained the social networks that held the neighborhood together. Some worked in domestic service, others in laundry facilities, cafeterias, or war-related support roles. Their labor—often invisible, always essential—ensured that families endured long years of uncertainty and sacrifice.

Throughout this period, the churches along First Avenue South remained the community's anchor. They prayed over departing soldiers, comforted families awaiting news, and organized assistance for those in need. Sunday services became moments of collective strength, where wartime anxieties were laid at the altar and hope was renewed. Pastors shared updates about local servicemen from the pulpit. Congregations rallied around families facing hardship, reinforcing the sense that no one endured the war alone.

The war years brought a fragile sense of progress. Savings accumulated where possible. Homes were improved. Institutions grew stronger. Yet beneath this stability lay constant pressure. Industrial accidents increased. Fatigue mounted. Racial discrimination remained entrenched. Black workers powered the war effort while remaining excluded from many of its rewards. Still, the South Community entered the mid-1940s grounded in resilience forged through decades of survival.

By the time victory was declared, Texas City stood transformed. Its industries were larger, its port busier, and its workforce hardened by years of nonstop production. For the South Community, World War II reshaped daily life, expanded opportunity, and deepened sacrifice. Families had endured separation, loss, and relentless labor, but they had also strengthened the institutions that defined the neighborhood.

The community emerged from the war carrying hope alongside exhaustion fragile stability built through shared effort and sustained by faith. That stability, however, would soon be tested by an event no one could have anticipated, an event that would forever alter the city and leave an indelible mark on the South Community.

The Texas City Disaster of 1947

By the mid-1940s, the South Community was holding on to a fragile but hard-earned stability. The Great Depression had tested families without breaking them. World War II had demanded sacrifice, long hours, and separation, but it had also brought steady work and a renewed sense of purpose. Along First Avenue South, families were rebuilding their lives, strengthening their churches, and imagining futures shaped by the progress they had fought to secure.

On the morning of April 16, 1947, that fragile stability was shattered.

What began as an ordinary workday at the Port of Texas City became the deadliest industrial accident in United States history—an explosion so violent that it reshaped the city, tore apart families, and left scars that would endure for generations. The disaster did not arrive with warning. It erupted into a city already awake, already working, already moving through the routines of daily life.

That morning, the French-registered vessel SS *Grandcamp* sat docked at the port, loaded with approximately 2,300 tons of ammonium nitrate, a chemical commonly used in fertilizer but dangerously explosive under certain conditions. The ship also carried small arms ammunition, twine, and machinery, a volatile combination stored within a confined hold. When a fire broke out below deck, thick smoke rose into the air and drifted across the waterfront. Onlookers gathered, unaware of the danger building beneath the surface.

Longshoremen, refinery workers, firefighters, and port laborers—many of them Black men from the South Community—moved toward the ship, not away from it. They were trained to respond. They were accustomed to risk. They were committed to their work and to one another. None could have imagined the scale of what was about to unfold.

At 9:12 a.m., the *Grandcamp* exploded.

The blast was catastrophic. It lifted the ship into the air, sent a shockwave across Galveston Bay, shattered windows miles away, and ignited fires throughout the industrial district. Buildings collapsed. Storage tanks ruptured. Railcars were hurled like toys. The explosion killed hundreds instantly—dockworkers, firefighters battling the blaze, and men laboring in nearby refineries. The official death toll exceeded five hundred, though historians agree the true number was likely higher, obscured by unrecorded contract labor and segregated reporting practices.

The South Community was struck with particular force. Many of the men assigned the most dangerous jobs—the jobs most readily available to Black workers in a segregated city—were on or near the docks that morning. In a single moment, families along First Avenue South lost fathers, brothers, sons, and uncles. Grief arrived without preparation, concentrated and overwhelming.

Yet even in devastation, the community responded as it always had.

They gathered.
They prayed.
They took care of one another.

The churches along First Avenue South—Barbour's Chapel, Galilee Methodist, and the nearby First Baptist—opened their doors immediately. They became places of refuge where families sought news, comfort, and shelter. Pastors moved from home to home, offering prayer and presence when words failed. Women organized food, clothing, and care for those who had lost everything. Children were shielded as best as possible from the trauma unfolding around them.

In the days that followed, fires continued to burn. The city struggled to identify the dead and account for the missing. Relief efforts were uneven and often segregated, leaving Black families to rely largely on their own institutions and networks for support. Funerals stretched on for weeks. Entire pews were filled with widows. Entire classrooms filled with children who would grow up without fathers.

The disaster altered more than the city's physical landscape. It reshaped the emotional terrain of the South Community. Loss was so concentrated, so sudden, and so profound that it became a defining memory passed down through generations. Families carried the names of the men they lost. Children grew up hearing stories of bravery, sacrifice, and the moment the sky broke open over Texas City.

And still, the community endured.

Homes were repaired. Lives were reorganized around absence. Churches strengthened their roles as centers of care and remembrance. Families raised children with the same discipline and determination that had carried them through every hardship before. The disaster revealed, once again, the depth of the South Community's resilience, a resilience rooted not in denial of loss, but in collective survival.

The Texas City Disaster of 1947 stands as one of the darkest chapters in the city's history. But for the South Community, it is also a testament to strength. They survived the unthinkable. They mourned together. They rebuilt together. And they carried forward the memory of those they lost, ensuring that their labor, their lives, and their sacrifices would never be forgotten.

Postwar Growth, Civil Rights, and Community Evolution

In the years following the Texas City Disaster of 1947, the South Community entered a period of rebuilding marked by grief, determination, and quiet resolve. Families who had lost loved ones carried their sorrow into daily life, finding strength in one another and in the institutions that had sustained them through every crisis before. Churches that had served as emergency centers during the disaster became places of healing, remembrance, and renewed purpose. Though shaken, the neighborhood refused to unravel.

The 1950s brought a gradual return to stability. Men who survived the disaster continued working in the refineries, rail yards, and port facilities that defined Texas City's industrial landscape. Postwar industrial expansion—driven by petrochemical growth, increased port traffic, and consolidation along the waterfront—created steady demand for labor. While working conditions remained dangerous and discrimination persisted, wages allowed many families to regain their footing. Homes were repaired. Gardens replanted. Small businesses reopened. Daily life resumed its familiar rhythm, shaped by habits of endurance learned over generations.

This period of recovery, however, unfolded alongside renewed military obligation. The Korean War (1950–1953) arrived just as families were beginning to stabilize after years of depression, war, and disaster. Once again, young men from the South Community were called to serve—some through enlistment, others through the draft. They left behind households still rebuilding, carrying with them the same mix of pride, fear, and uncertainty that had accompanied earlier wars.

Military service during the Korean War brought mixed consequences. For some families, steady military pay offered financial support in a city where industrial labor remained unpredictable and hazardous. For others, service meant prolonged separation and anxiety, layered onto losses that were still fresh. Letters home were read aloud in kitchens and church gatherings, folded carefully, and saved alongside earlier wartime correspondence. Korea became part of the community's shared experience, spoken of quietly but remembered clearly.

As the decade progressed, Texas City expanded outward, but the South Community remained a world unto itself. Children walked to school. Neighbors shared food, news, and responsibility. Churches along First Avenue South continued to anchor spiritual and social life. Sunday mornings filled the avenue with families dressed in their best. Weeknights glowed with choir rehearsals, prayer meetings, youth programs, and women's circles. These routines reinforced continuity in a city undergoing rapid change.

The 1960s ushered in a period of profound transformation. The civil-rights movement reshaped national consciousness, and its effects reached Texas City as well. School desegregation began in the mid-1960s, altering educational life for families who had long relied on Booker T. Washington School as the center of Black learning. Children who once attended segregated classrooms entered integrated schools across the city, navigating unfamiliar environments with the discipline, confidence, and self-worth instilled by families, teachers, and churches.

At the same time, the Vietnam War emerged as a defining force in community life. Stretching from the late 1950s through the mid-1970s, the conflict overlapped directly with the civil-rights era. Young men from the South Community served in increasing numbers, many drafted into a war that divided the nation. Families watched sons, brothers, and husbands leave a city still shaped by segregation, even as they were asked to fight for democratic ideals abroad. The contradiction was neither abstract nor ignored.

Vietnam reshaped the community in lasting ways. Some veterans returned carrying visible injuries and invisible wounds. Others used military service as a pathway into education, skilled trades, or relocation through the GI Bill and related benefits. Military service became one of several forces contributing to the gradual dispersal of families beyond the original neighborhood, linking war directly to later patterns of migration, opportunity, and change.

Through Korea and Vietnam, the South Community continued a long tradition of service to a nation that did not always serve them in return. These wars became part of the community's shared memories spoken of in churches, remembered at family gatherings, and carried forward in the lives of those who served and those who waited for them to return.

During the 1970s and 1980s, the community entered another phase of evolution. Expanded housing options, economic mobility, military benefits, and the long-term effects of integration led some families to move into new neighborhoods across Texas City and beyond. Others relocated to Houston, Dallas, Austin, California, or the Midwest, following work, education, and opportunity. This gradual dispersal mirrored broader patterns of Black American migration across the Gulf Coast.

Yet even as families spread outward, the South Community remained the center of gravity. People returned for church anniversaries, funerals, weddings, and reunions. They returned for Easter Sundays, Christmas programs, and summer revivals. Elders became living archives, carrying memories of migration, worship, education, military service, and survival. Their stories grounded younger generations in a lineage of endurance and pride.

By the late twentieth century, the South Community had become both a place and a legacy. Its influence extended far beyond its original footprint. Descendants carried its values into workplaces, churches, civic roles, and families of their own. What had been built within a segregated neighborhood continued to shape lives across generations and geographies.

These postwar decades were defined not by stasis, but by adaptation. The South Community evolved as the world changed around it, shaped by recovery, civil rights, military service, and migration. Through every transition, its foundation remained intact—faith, family, work, and collective responsibility. The community grew without forgetting who it was.

Legacy, Memory, and the Diaspora of the South Community

By the late 1970s and into the 1980s, the South Community stood at a quiet turning point. The neighborhood still lived. Churches still rang with Sunday hymns. Elders who had built the community with their own hands remained present, visible, and active. Children and grandchildren still returned home after school, after work, after long weeks away. Yet change was unmistakable. Homes stood farther apart. Familiar faces were fewer. The community was thinning—not erased, not gone, but beginning to stretch beyond its original boundaries.

The 1980s were not a period of disappearance; they were a period of living continuity under pressure. Families still gathered along First Avenue South. Church anniversaries, funerals, weddings, and reunions continued to anchor collective life. Elders told stories not as history lessons, but as lived memory—accounts of migration, labor, worship, and survival passed across kitchen tables and church pews. Memory was still embodied, still spoken, still held by those who had lived it.

At the same time, younger generations were increasingly pulled outward. Economic opportunity, education, military service, and housing availability drew families into new neighborhoods across Texas City and into surrounding regions. This outward movement did not signal abandonment. It marked the beginning of what would become a diaspora—a widening circle of descendants who carried the values of the South Community with them even as they lived elsewhere.

The 1990s deepened this transition. As elders aged, responsibility for memory shifted subtly but decisively. Sons and daughters became caretakers not only of people, but of stories. The physical neighborhood continued to thin as industrial pressure intensified, and investment flowed away from residential preservation. Yet the community remained connected through churches, family networks, and ritual return. People came home for milestone events, even if they no longer lived within the old footprint.

Military service remained part of that generational story. During the Gulf War (1990–1991), men and women from South Community families once again served in uniform. Though the conflict was shorter than earlier wars, its presence reinforced a long tradition of service that stretched across generations—from World War I through Vietnam and into the late twentieth century. Military service continued to shape mobility, opportunity, and identity, linking the South Community's past to its evolving future.

As the century turned, the early 2000s brought sharper clarity about what was being lost. Elders who had once carried memory effortlessly now carried it with urgency. Churches faced relocation, consolidation, or closure, and long-standing homes disappeared from the landscape.

At Barbour's Chapel Baptist Church, this moment marked a transition rather than a sudden disappearance. On August 26, 2001, Reverend James E. Brown, Sr. was called to the church, bringing with him a vision to build a new sanctuary that could carry the congregation forward. The property along E. F. Lowry Expressway was sold, and land was purchased at 7420 FM 1765. A groundbreaking ceremony for the new church edifice was held on March 15, 2003, and the first worship service in the new building took place on April 15, 2004. The formal crossover processional and services were completed on April 24, 2005, marking the congregation's full transition into its new home.

Because of this transition, the year 2005 is often cited in secondary sources and oral histories as the demolition date of Barbour's Chapel's historic structure on First Avenue South. However, primary photographic evidence taken in 2015 confirms that the brick, towered sanctuary remained standing at least a decade later. This discrepancy indicates that the 2005 date reflects the congregation's relocation rather than the immediate removal of the historic building. The 2015 photographs—along with the presence of the 1973 elevator plaque and the removed cornerstone—establish that the brick sanctuary remained intact into the early twenty-first century, even after it ceased functioning as the active church home.

In this way, Barbour's Chapel did not disappear abruptly. Its congregation moved forward, while its historic structure lingered on the landscape—an enduring but vulnerable physical anchor of memory during a period of transition, uncertainty, and loss.

By the 2010s, descendants, church leaders, educators, and community advocates began organizing memory deliberately. The opening of the Sanders/Vincent Community Center in 2010 represented continuity between education, leadership, and legacy. It stood as a declaration that the South Community's history would not vanish quietly. Efforts to document oral histories, gather photographs, and preserve artifacts accelerated as elders aged and the risk of loss became undeniable.

These preservation efforts culminated in the creation of the Black American Cultural Park, built on sacred ground. The park preserved the cornerstone and bell of Barbour's Chapel, transforming remnants of loss into symbols of endurance. It marked a shift from living memory alone to intentional archives from stories remembered to history protected.

The arrival of COVID-19 in 2020 intensified that urgency. The pandemic struck at the heart of the community's living archive. Elders—long the keepers of memory—were among the most vulnerable. Losses came quickly, sometimes without the chance for final conversations or recorded testimony. COVID exposed what had long been true but not always spoken aloud: that memory, if not preserved, could vanish within a generation.

In response, descendants acted. Phone calls replaced visits. Stories were written down. Photographs were scanned. Names were recorded. Memory became an act of preservation rather than recollection alone. The South Community's legacy entered a new phase, only lived, not only remembered, but actively safeguarded.

Today, the South Community exists as both place and presence. Its physical footprint has narrowed, but its influence has widened. Descendants carry their values into churches, workplaces, civic roles, and families across Texas and beyond. The community lives on in reunions, in anniversaries, in the African American Cultural Park, and in the determination of those who refuse to let its story be erased.

This chapter marks that transition, from neighborhood to lineage, from lived space to remembered ground. It tells the story of a people who adapted without forgetting, who dispersed without disappearing, and who carried their history forward even as the land beneath it changed. The South Community did not fade. It transformed, and in that transformation, it endured.

Erasure, Green Space, and the Fight for Memory

By the end of the twentieth century, the South Community—once a vibrant, self-sustaining, ten-block neighborhood anchored by First Avenue South, began to disappear from the physical landscape of Texas City. The change did not happen overnight. It unfolded gradually, often quietly, and frequently without public acknowledgment. But for the families who had lived there for generations, the transformation was unmistakable. Homes vanished. Churches were demolished. Businesses closed. Streets emptied. And the land that had once held the heart of Black Texas City was redefined as something else.

The city called it green space.

To understand this erasure, it is necessary to understand the forces that shaped it. For decades, the South Community existed within the shadow of Texas City's industrial corridor. Refineries, chemical plants, rail lines, and port facilities surrounded the neighborhood on all sides. As the city expanded through the 1980s and 1990s, industrial interests gained increasing influence over zoning and land-use decisions. Planning maps from the late twentieth century show a steady shift: parcels once occupied by homes were reclassified for industrial use, left unzoned, or designated as buffers between residential areas and expanding facilities.

These decisions were rarely framed as displacement. Instead, they were presented as progress, safety, or environmental management. Yet their effects were cumulative and uneven. Investment flowed away from residential preservation. The infrastructure aged without repair. City services withdrew gradually. Families who had lived side by side for generations found themselves isolated as neighbors moved away or properties were acquired and cleared.

The South Community—already limited in political power and representation—became increasingly vulnerable to decisions made beyond its control.

Homes that had stood for decades were purchased, condemned, or left to deteriorate. As conditions worsened, some families relocated by necessity rather than choice. Others held on as long as possible, refusing to leave land where parents and grandparents were buried, baptized, and remembered. Streets that once echoed with children's voices grew quiet. Density thinned until only fragments of the neighborhood remained.

The churches that had anchored First Avenue South were not spared.

Galilee Methodist Church relocated.

First Baptist shifted its center of gravity.

And in 2005, Barbour's Chapel Baptist Church—the spiritual heart of the avenue—was demolished.

The loss of Barbour's Chapel marked a turning point. It was not simply the destruction of a building. It was the removal of a sanctuary where generations had been baptized, married, mourned, and sustained one another through segregation, disaster, and change. It was the place where families gathered after the Texas City Disaster of 1947, where relief was organized when no other support was offered, and where children learned the values that shaped their lives. When the church fell, a piece of the community's spiritual architecture fell with it.

In the years that followed, the land where homes and churches once stood was cleared. Grass replaced foundations. Open fields replaced neighborhoods. The city described this transformation as green space—language that suggested renewal, openness, and environmental benefit. But for descendants of the South Community, the green space told a different story.

It was absence.
It was silence.
It was erasure.

Green space became a euphemism for displacement, a way to beautify land while burying the history that had unfolded there. The open fields did not speak of labor, worship, survival, or joy.

They did not reveal the lives of the men who died in the 1947 disaster or the women who held families together through decades of hardship. They did not acknowledge the institutions that once gave the neighborhood coherence and meaning.

The land was green, but the memory was not.

Yet even as the physical structures disappeared, the people refused to let the story die. Descendants carried history in photographs, oral traditions, church programs, and family memory. Elders spoke of what once stood where grass now grew. They traced property lines from memory. They named families who had lived on streets no longer marked. They understood a truth the city's maps did not show: the South Community was not erased, it was displaced.

Displacement did not dissolve lineage.

By the late 1990s and early 2000s, the fight for memory had become a new chapter in the community's story. Descendants, church leaders, historians, and advocates began gathering documents, photographs, and testimonies. They reconstructed family histories. They documented churches, schools, and businesses that no longer stood. They challenged the narrative that framed the neighborhood's disappearance as inevitable or benign.

These efforts aligned with broader movements across Texas to preserve Black American cemeteries, freedom colonies, and historic neighborhoods threatened by industrial expansion and redevelopment. But for the South Community, the work was personal. It was about reclaiming truth from silence.

That work culminated in the creation of the African American Cultural Park, built on sacred ground. The park preserved the cornerstone and bell of Barbour's Chapel, physical remnants that survived demolition and now stand as symbols of endurance. It transformed green space into a site of memory, testimony, and resistance.

The park does more than commemorate loss. It counters erasure. It tells the story that the open fields tried to hide. It names the families who built the South Community. It honors the churches that shaped their

spiritual life. It remembers the school that educated its children. It acknowledges the disaster that tested its strength. And it confronts the displacement that followed.
Erasure removed structures.

It did not remove people.
It did not remove legacy.
It did not remove truth.

The South Community endures—not because the city preserved it, but because its descendants refused to let it disappear. This chapter marks that refusal. It names the forces that erased a neighborhood and the determination that ensured its memory would survive.

Legacy Preservation and Institutional Memory

As the physical landscape of the South Community continued to disappear in the early twenty-first century, memory itself became contested ground. Homes were gone. Churches had been demolished or relocated. Streets that once carried the rhythms of daily life were no longer marked by the people who built them. What remained was not emptiness, but vulnerability—the risk that a community's history could be flattened into silence once its structures were removed.

For elders who had lived the story, memory still resided in the body. They could point to where homes once stood, name families who lived on blocks now covered in grass, and recount events with the clarity of lived experience. But time was changing that reality. As the 2000s progressed, the question was no longer whether the South Community mattered. The question was whether its story would survive beyond those who could still speak it aloud.

Preservation did not begin as a formal project. It began as an urgency.

Families began gathering photographs before they were lost. Church anniversary programs were pulled from drawers and boxes. Stories once told casually were repeated with intention. Descendants asked elders to name dates, places, and people. Memory began shifting from something assumed to something deliberately protected.

This shift marked the beginning of institutional memory. One of the most significant expressions of that transition was the creation of the Sanders/Vincent Community Center, which opened in 2010. Built on the historic site of Booker T. Washington School, the center symbolized continuity between education, leadership, and legacy. It carried forward the names of George Burr Sanders and Calvin Vincent, educators whose influence had shaped generations. The center did more than provide space. It anchored memory to place, ensuring that the values cultivated within the South Community remained visible and accessible.

During the 2010s, preservation efforts gained momentum. Descendants, church leaders, educators, and community advocates organized with greater clarity and purpose. Oral histories were recorded. Artifacts were collected. Public recognition was pursued not as validation, but as protection. These efforts reflected a growing awareness that memory, once lost, could not be recovered.

The creation of the African American Cultural Park represented the most visible outcome of this work. Built on land once defined as green space, the park reclaimed that ground as sacred. The preservation of Barbour's Chapel's cornerstone and bell transformed fragments of loss into enduring testimony. The park became a counter-archive—an answer to erasure that insisted on presence, naming, and truth.

Institutional memory did not replace lived memory; it extended it. It ensured that future generations would encounter the South Community not as rumor or footnote, but as history grounded in evidence, voice, and place. The park, the community center, and the growing body of recorded testimony formed a network of remembrance that resisted disappearance.

Yet even as preservation advanced, urgency deepened.

By the late 2010s, elders who carried firsthand knowledge of the community's earliest chapters were aging. Each loss represented more than personal grief; it represented the disappearance of unrecorded history. The work of preservation became time-sensitive. Memory could no longer wait.

That reality was made unmistakably clear with the arrival of COVID-19 in 2020.

The pandemic struck at the heart of the South Community's living archive. Elders—long the keepers of memory—were among the most vulnerable. Losses came swiftly and, at times, without the opportunity for final conversations or recorded testimony. COVID transformed preservation from an act of care into an act of emergency.

In response, descendants intensified their efforts. Stories were written down. Photographs were digitized. Names were documented. What had once been shared orally was captured intentionally. Memory became collective responsibility, not an individual burden.

Today, the legacy of the South Community is held across multiple forms—living memory, institutional record, and public space. It resides in the African American Cultural Park, in the Sanders/Vincent Community Center, in church archives, in family collections, and in the determination of those who refuse to allow the community's history to fade.

Institutional memory does not freeze the South Community in time. It carries it forward. It ensures that the story remains dynamic, truthful, and accessible—not only to descendants, but to the city that grew around it.

This chapter marks that transformation. It tells the story of how a community confronted erasure by building memory strong enough to endure beyond physical loss. It affirms that preservation is not about looking backward, but about protecting truth so it can move forward—intact, visible, and unbroken.

The South Community Lives On Continuity, Responsibility, and the Present Moment

Today, the South Community no longer exists as it once did on the physical landscape of Texas City. The houses are gone. The streets are quiet. The churches that once lined First Avenue South have been demolished, relocated, or transformed. What remains is not the neighborhood as it was, but the community as it endures.

The South Community lives on through people.

It lives in descendants who carry its values into their own families, churches, and civic lives. It lives in the elders whose stories shaped generations and whose memories continue to guide those who came after them. It lives in the African American Cultural Park, in the Sanders/Vincent Community Center, and in the records, photographs, and oral histories gathered with care and intention. It lives wherever someone remembers where they came from—and why it matters.

The work of preservation did not end with recognition. Public markers, memorials, and institutions provided visibility, but they did not complete the task. Memory is not static. It requires stewardship. Each generation inherits not only the benefits of what was built, but the responsibility to protect what remains.

That responsibility became especially clear in the 2020s.

The arrival of COVID-19 exposed how fragile living memory could be. Elders who carried firsthand knowledge of the South Community's earliest chapters were among the most vulnerable. Losses came quickly. Stories that had not yet been recorded disappeared with them. The

pandemic revealed an urgent truth: history can be lost not only through demolition and displacement, but through time itself.
In response, descendants acted with renewed determination. Preservation became active rather than aspirational. Family stories were documented. Names were written down. Photographs were scanned. Conversations once assumed were recorded intentionally. Memory shifted from inheritance to obligation.

This moment did not weaken the South Community's legacy—it clarified it.

The South Community has never been defined solely by geography. From its earliest days, it was shaped by faith, labor, mutual responsibility, and collective care. Those values survived the Great Depression. They endured world wars, hurricanes, and industrial disasters. They carried families through segregation, displacement, and erasure. And they continue to guide descendants navigating the present.

The story of the South Community is not a story of loss alone. It is a story of creation, endurance, and refusal. Refusal to disappear quietly. Refusal to allow history to be flattened or forgotten. Refusal to let green space replace truth.

This manuscript does not exist to mourn what was destroyed. It exists to name what was built—and what continues to matter.

The South Community mattered because people built it with intention in a world that denied them space. It mattered because they labored in dangerous industries while nurturing children, faith, and dignity at home. It mattered because they created institutions when none were provided. And it matters now because its descendants insist that history be remembered honestly and fully.

The work continues.

As elders pass, as cities change, and as time moves forward, the responsibility to remember does not fade deepen. The South Community lives on wherever its story is told with care, accuracy, and respect. It lives on in the refusal to allow erasure to become the final word.

This is not the end of the story.
It is the continuation of a lineage.

And as long as that lineage is remembered, the South Community endures.

Displacement

Displacement did not arrive in Texas City as a single decision or a clearly marked moment. It unfolded gradually, through a narrowing of options that made remaining increasingly difficult for the families of the South Community. What had once been a stable, intergenerational neighborhood began to loosen—not because residents abandoned it, but because the conditions that allowed it to function were steadily removed.

The first changes were often subtle. Individual homes were sold or condemned. Properties once maintained by extended families fell into disrepair as resources thinned and uncertainty grew. Some residents left by necessity rather than choice, relocating to other parts of the city or beyond in search of housing that felt more secure. Others remained, determined to hold on as long as possible to land where parents and grandparents had lived, worshiped, and been buried.

Displacement did not happen evenly. Some families left early, sensing that the neighborhood's future was becoming increasingly fragile. Others stayed for decades, adapting to worsening conditions while maintaining routines shaped by faith, kinship, and memory. The South Community did not empty all at once; it thinned. Familiar faces disappeared gradually. Homes stood farther apart. The density that had once provided protection and mutual care began to dissolve.

As residential life weakened, institutions felt the strain. Churches that had anchored First Avenue South faced difficult decisions. Declining membership, shifting populations, and increasing pressure from surrounding development forced congregations to consider relocation, consolidation, or closure. Each move carried emotional weight. Leaving was never simply logistical; it meant severing ties to sacred ground consecrated by generations of worship, labor, and survival.

Displacement was reinforced by the withdrawal of support. Infrastructure improvements bypassed the neighborhood. Services diminished. Investment flowed elsewhere. The absence of repair and maintenance made daily life more difficult, further narrowing the possibilities for families who remained. What had once been framed as a temporary inconvenience became long-term instability.

Importantly, displacement was not framed by the city as loss. It was described through neutral language, development, expansion, safety, and efficiency. Yet for residents, the consequences were deeply personal. Homes were not interchangeable. Streets were not empty space. Each departure represented the unraveling of relationships built over decades.

Even as physical presence diminished, the community did not disappear. Families carried the South Community with them into new neighborhoods and new cities. Churches remained centers of return, drawing descendants back for anniversaries, funerals, and reunions. Memory traveled where people went. Displacement removed people from place, but it did not erase identity.

This chapter marks the moment when staying became increasingly untenable—not because the community failed, but because the ground beneath it was steadily taken away. Displacement was not an accident. It was the outcome of pressure finally made physical.

What followed would be described as renewal, green space, or progress. Before land was cleared and renamed, it was dismantled family by family, block by block, memory by memory.

From Narrative to Record

The material that follows reproduces and documents text, names, and commemorative language preserved in the African American Cultural Park. This content is presented as artifact and institutional memory, retained in its original form to honor the community's record of itself.

What follows marks a deliberate shift in form and authority.
Up to this point, the history of the South Community has been traced through narrative synthesis—drawing from oral histories, institutional records, municipal documentation, and lived experience to explain how a neighborhood was built, sustained, pressured, and ultimately displaced. The African American Cultural Park represents the moment when that history was no longer interpreted but physically asserted. The park exists because the community's original landscape was removed. Its inscriptions, lists, and commemorative texts were placed into the ground as a response to erasure, an act of preservation that fixed memory where buildings, streets, and institutions once stood.

These materials were not created for publication or analysis. They were created for presence, recognition, and survival.

AFRICAN AMERICAN CULTURAL PARK

African American Historical Cultural Park Creator

Lynn Ray Ellison, Ed.D., Commissioner Emeritus
City of Texas City, Texas

I was born and raised in Texas City, Texas, from my birth in 1941 on First Avenue South (MLK). Let me acknowledge first the Mayor, Matthew T. Doyle, the 2019 City Commissioners, and Parks and Recreation Director, Dennis J. Harris, for their total support on this project. A very good friend of mine, who we totally love, served over 50 years of service to the City of Texas City. He was former Mayor Charles T. "Chuck" Doyle, who drove me around, and we selected the site. Plus, he added more history to the park by saying, "Let's add a full-size picture of Martin Luther King, Jr., and I and my wife, Mary Ellen Doyle, will pay for the statue that will be erected in the middle of the park." I thank all of these people and others because my heart is totally in making Texas City a better place to live, work, worship, and play.

Few things about me, I was one of the first two commissioners that were elected to Texas City's new government in 1978, the other one being the late Thomas F. Carter, Sr., from that tenure from 1978 – 2000. I am the longest-serving, straight commissioner in the history of Texas City,

Texas. So, I have been a politician, historian, activist, motivator, mentor, playwright, journalist, former high school teacher, college teacher, and coach. I continue to mentor African American athletes by networking with recruiters at historically black colleges and others, ensuring their academic success. I, along with countless other former Booker T. Washington students, have always had a strong passion for our former school since it was closed in 1967. We are scattered now throughout the city, county, across the states, and points beyond. Our organization, the B.T.W Ex's, has been in existence for nearly 40 years, and we are the driving force behind the projects. In 2006, we delayed this project to help get recognition to all the African American schools that were closed due to integration. In 2009, we accomplished our goal through the Texas Legislature of the state of Texas. Now, all these once black schools are recognized for their history, legacy, achievements, honors, awards, outstanding teachers, and students in the archives of Texas History.

This historical cultural park is one of four across the State of Texas in Austin, San Antonio, Houston, and now Texas City. The purpose of this project is to dedicate, respect, and honor all the people who lived in this original African American community since Texas City was incorporated in 1911. When African Americans first came to Texas City

as ward, there were no encouragements for them to settle/here. The need for labor on the docks, waterfronts, construction of Texas Refineries, and other major industries made their need necessary. We honor our parents, pastors, ministers, friends, neighbors, as well as others who came from cotton gin workers, watermen, pool room owners, saw mill towns, corn fields, cane fields, rice, and tobacco fields, from incarnation, off Texas Avenue at the north, from Bay Street on the East, from 10th Street on the west, and 4th Avenue on the south; this sacred community of 10 square blocks is known as our "Mecca." This project represents all those individuals and families who settled, worked, and raised families in the sacred and now beloved community of Texas City, Texas.

Lynn Ray Ellison, Ed.D
Commissioner Emeritus

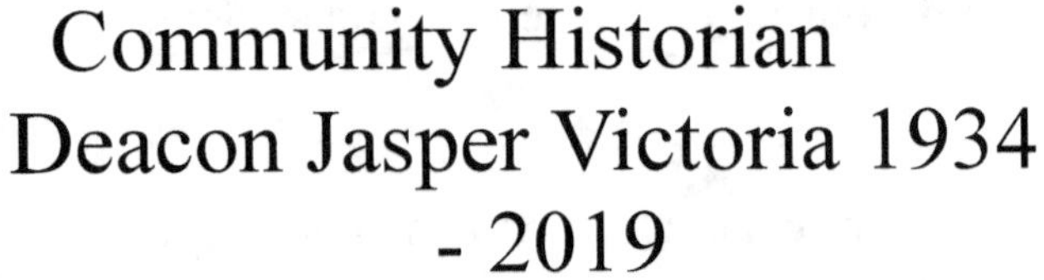

Community Historian Deacon Jasper Victoria 1934 - 2019

The African American Historical Committee would like to acknowledge Deacon Jasper Victoria. The complete history of this park could not have been possible if it wasn't for, in many instances, Brother Victoria's firsthand knowledge of the physical, social, political, and religious history of the 10-block segregated community in the City of Texas City.

Our community, in which African Americans lived in Texas City, beginning in 1941, when Texas City was incorporated as a town, later a small city. Deacon Jasper Victoria was in the graduating class of 1953 at Booker T. Washington High School here in Texas City. Shortly after, Jasper joined the Texas Avenue church. Victoria possessed great knowledge of our African American history from the 1930's to the present. He remembered the names of the people, their families, church, schoolmates, classmates, and the location of homes and most, if not all, the 504 families that lived in the 10-block rectangle bordered by Texas Avenue to the North, 10th Street to the West, Fourth Avenue to the South, and 5th Street to the East. So, we salute Deacon Jasper Victoria and his wife Dorothy, their children, grandchildren, and great-grandchildren, for his historical knowledge. Until his passing in 2019, he was very active in his community in service, school, religious, and political activities. He and his wife attended New Macedonia Baptist Church in Hitchcock, Texas, where Rev. Kimble was pastor. We salute Deacon Victoria, a lifelong Texas Citian, for his endeavors.

Lynn Ray Ellison, Ed.D
Commissioner Emeritus

504 Freedmen families settled, owned and operated businesses, attended Booker T Washington School, worked, worshipped at six churches, and raised their families within ten square blocks of Texas City, from Texas Avenue on the North, 10th Street on the West, Bay Street on the East, and Fourth Avenue on the South.

Otis and Irene McKinney Moses
Henry and Odessa Randle Sanford
Clarence and Pearl Godfrey
James and Ethel Brooks
Joseph (Jim) and Alice Hardy
Reverend Thurman W, and Helen Griffin Medlock
Morris and Johnnie Mae Davis
Clarence and Mattie Young Bradley
Dorothea, George, and Evelyn Jolly
Clydie and Lucille Erskin
Wesley, Geneva, Andrus, and Leslie Andrus, Jr.
Gertrude Taylor, Laurence, and Jo Ann Taylor
Willis Jr. and Lela Martin
Acie and Essie Jones
Blanche, Columbus Smith, and Verna Hill
Leroy Sr., Alginore Gary Grocery Store
Haywood and Aslee Hart
Ruby Hart Autry and Jean Hart Martin
Ethan and Ethel Payne
Nathaniel and Sadie Mayes
Johnnie and Bessie Young
David, Dora, and Barbara Brooks
Doris J. Conley and Dorothy M. Murphy
Reverend T.H. Giles Sr. and Lela Kimble Giles
Paul G., Myrtle Giles, and Debra Davis
George Sr. and Sarah Mae Reason
Orris Sr. and Katie Johnson
Charles Sr. and Novella Anderson
Francis and Lucy T. Boston
Richard, Lucinda Mayes, and Jessie Wise, Irene Adams, and Adonis Jones
Evelyn Alexander Parker
Mr. Simon and Reverend Sadie Cleveland
M. Allean Cunguness Pettit
Willie and Dorothy Burnett
Mrs. Ida Guss and William Patin
Willie/Eva and James Lee
Griggs Sr. and Johnnie Mae Owens
Clomer, Polly, and Verdell Earls
Jesse and Sallie Walker, Jr.
Levi Sr. and Fannie Haddock
Robert and Ida Goldman
Suddie Jones and Bessie A. Sherwood
Dan and Hattie M. Griffin
David, Dora, and Exia Porter
Clifton and Josie Matthews Wade
Lena Bell and Leon Norris
PaPa Beamer/Margarita

Tyler Thomas Jr./The Midnight Dream Café
Ruby Lee Greer
Lionell and Barbara McCray
Jim Woodkins Jr. and Christa Woodkins
Louis and Willie Mae Parker
Otis and Veola Sims Randle
L.A. and Flossie L. Holmes
Alfred W. and Curtis James Duhon
Harry and Hazel A. Williams
Annie Mae Payne
Lucis and Elnora Tryals
Johnnie and Sarah Howard
Ethel K. Mock *Ms. Lil Bit*
Lacy and Beatrice James
Reverend Earnest Sr. *P.D.* and Artis Wisby
Vivian Scott, Rubin, and Eddie V. Carter
John H. Sr. and Ester Reed
Rosetta Coleman Jackson
Alonzo Sr. and Tennessee Wiley
John D. Estelle Bedford
Thadus and Mamie Owens
Buster and Flonnie Lewis
Wilbur and Patricia Lewis
James H. and Zonobia C. Williams
Jay A. and Glenda R. Williams
Cozy and Hosa Brown
James *Buster* Laruth Griffin
Robert Sr. and Gladys M. Griffin
Phil E. and Ollie Griffin Grant
Ned and Ruby Ellison
Myra Louise Beavers Britton
Lewis T. and Rena Mae Adams
Osie V. Sr. and Anna Combs
Bowman and Jessie L. Perkins
Reverend Ellis and Loleta Johnson
Annie Bell Bogan and Martha Woolridge
Reverend Marshal Sr. and Minnie Kimble
Martha and Earl Payne
Billie *Jim* Estelle Griffin
Denis Delany and Ester Griffin
Mable Lacass and Alfred Brown
Callie and Lloyd Richards
Charles C. and Stella B. Jones
Harry and Lallie James
Emma and Mrs. Harris Jones
F.D. and Martha Evans
Frank and Gladys Evans
Phillip and Johnny Mae Meyers
Robert and Annie Gordon
Leslie and Lillie B. Caldwell
Wallace and Eliza Henry
Melvin *Speck* Griffin/Gregory
Charles and Clara Butler Gates
J.D. Stephens and Robert Payne
Maurice and Elouise Goldman
Oliver Sr. and Elnora Swan
Reece and Irma Jean Moore Fonteno
Junious James and Ruby Mae Lewis
Lee Roy and Hazel Hardy

Pink and Allie Williams
Gregory and Rita Hardy
Charley and Dorothy Kimble
Roberson
Earnest Sr. and Gloria Rhem
Parker
Rose Lewis Kimble
Euric Socs Mannie Mae Phillips
Richard and Willetta Mayes
Booker T. Augusta Johnson
Lucille and Clarence Artis
Henderson and Juanita Johnson
Johonnie and Asie Lee McDaniels
Eddie Lee and Elizabeth Johnson
James and Gaberial Lena Scott
Nadine and Betty Archie Scott
Laurence Murray
Russell Sr. and Heneritta Rice
Willie Lee and Isalee Young
Dorothea Jones
Mrs. Clara's Store
Earl Sr. and Pearline King
Reverend James Perryman GMC
Reverend F.M. Johnson FBC
Reverend James H. Scott BCBC
Reverend L.B. Brown GMBC
Reverend Thomas A. Lee MZBC
John and Cenia Anderson's
Kindergarten

Eli and Beatrice Henry
Sam and Hattie Coverson
Richard Felder Sr.
William Fuller
Eva Wilson and L.C. Calton
Joe and Essie Mitchell
Lonnie and Evelyn McClure
Arnell/Rhem
George and Dez Eden
Earnest Sr. and Georgia Caldwell
Billie Faye Henry Murray
Sedalia Phillips Beavers
Lillian Peterson
Budwines/Longs
Arthur and Viola Miles
Harold Weaver and Louis Thomas
Ollie and Margaret Waters
Ceary and Sugar Johnson
Wealthy Davis
Tom Edwards
Delores Williams Sneed
Moore's Café
Jay's Inn
Melvin Griffin/Mary Francis
Booker/Stanley
Booker T. Washington School
Homer Sr. and John L. Rollins

Charles Brown (Famous Blues Singer)
Moses / Mattie Simpson Brown
Alice Simpson Matthew / Jerry Simpson
Dorothy Sanford
E.L. Matthew
Agnes Gordon / Christine Gordon
Robert L. Gordon
Lee R. Gordon
Howard Lawrence McAfee
Annie Ruth McAfee
Jeff Fletcher, Sr. / Ellese Fletcher
Lottie Rebecca Reason
Sara Pearl Reason
George M.R. Reason, Jr.
Samuel E.M. Reason
Barbara Martin Jones
Vera Martin Horton
Alice Cleveland / Emma
Allean Cunguness
Levi Haddock, Sr. / Hazel Haddock
Rev. McCloud Family
Tom Jarmon
Ella Jarmon
Ella Jarmon Todd
W.C. / Doll Howard
Clifton Sr. / Mae Pearl Jones
Al Jay / Annie Jones
Willie Earl Martin
Robert "Rev" Martin
Randolph Scott
Janice Collins
Frederick Lewis Combs
Ossie V. Combs, Jr. (U.S. Navy ADM)
Adjurale Combs Heard
Ida Ruth Dims Gates
Junell Sims Drisdale
Kenny Arnold / Calvin Arnold
Willetta Brooks Price
Ruth Earl Waters (Famous Singer)
Ollie Cash
Marvin "Hannibal" Peterson (Famous Musician)
Iverson Godfrey, Sr.
Lee Andrew Giles
Sarah Godfrey Giles
Edward Williams
Mary Elizabeth Williams
Robert Lee Williams, Jr.
George Jr. / Cora Cash
Elnora Brown Brooks
Alfred Leon Brown, Jr.
Jack / Marcia Ellison
Robert Goldman, Jr.
Willie Faye Thomas
Earl Parker
Mary Lee Parker
Emmitt Parker
Louis Parker, Jr.
Hattie Mae Owens
Johnnie Ray Owens
Billy Gene Owens
David Earl Owens
Mammie Easter Owens
W.L. / Mattie Craddock
Bruce / Sherri Sr. Ellison
Gail / Gertrude Ellison
Patrick Renard Brown
Karen Alicia Brown
Richard Taylor Sr.
Victoria Phelps Taylor
Norris Lee Williams
Gwendolyn Williams
Velma Sanders

Clyde / Eddie / Jet Johnsons
Leo Williams / Margaret Williams
Stella Miller
Carl Dean Tryals
Jewel Marie Young Hunter
James Henderson
Myrtle Henderson
Alma Causey
Ann / Milton Jackson, Sr.
The Dawson Family
Edward Lee Gates
Dorothy Barrett Murphy
McNeil Barrett
Roger B. Barrett
Doris Jean Barrett Conley
Eddie / Henry / Edrick Caldwell
John / Charles Ellison
Lillie B. Dorris
Lillie M. Pointer
Doris Widgee Scott
James E. Beasley / Joseph Pointer
Lee / Frankie Sims
Matthew / Minnie Todd
Bessie / James / Kenneth Adams
Warren / Henretta Jones
Eugene "Plato" Simpson
James / Ruth Porter
Pinky Warren / Annie Mae Parker
Theodore / Arma Craddock
Joe / Johnnie B Cofield
Morrolinne Davis Haddock
Myrtle Rice / Elnora Graham
Willie Cole / Fred Monroe
Eddie Jenning / George Eden
Larry Scott
Willie "Duke" James
Earlean King
Vivian King
Earl Leon King
Etheatre Mayes
Ethel Scott McFarland
J.W. Scott / Shirley French
Rufus Hood (KIA Vietnam 1968)
Elnora / Evelyn Hogan
Ray Dell Jones
Jewel Hood / Betty Hill
Robert Cofield / Roy Williams
Joe Caldwell (All-Pro NBA)
Jessie McCutchen
Bobbie Simpson
Griggs Owens / Betty Clay

Myrtle Giles Davis
Dorothy House Godfrey
Billie Faye Murray
Julia Butler
Gabrieliana Scott
Myrtle Jermany Seales
Marie N. Williams
Lois McCloud Davenport
Annie M. Simpson Owens
Rosa Eelbeck
Aurilla D. Beaves
Ethel B. Vincent
Willia Bonner
Evelyn McClure
Cecile J. Johnson
Ora L. Carter
Janie M. Johnson
Inez Ricks
Theresa Preacher
Barbara Cooper
Ida M. Callier
Freddie Niles (Coach)
Winfred Bonner
Lawrence Worsham
Thomas T. Carter Jr. (Coach)
Iverson Godfrey, Jr. (Coach)
Albert Dickson, Jr.
James A. Wilson
Jessie McFarland
Charles Granger
Charles Sorians
Myrna Nichols
Audrey Rice
Delores Frazier
B.T.W. P.T.A. Presidents
Ethel Brown
Ruth Toland
Helen Malone
Mamie Amy
Vivian Carter
Mary A. Payne
Sgt. Dorsey (WW1)
James Beasley
Marci Johnson Simmons
Ronald Douglas Alford
Doris Jean Alford
Arnell / Carolyn Crayton
Charlie Jackson, Jr.
Rosemary Jackson
Annie Pearl Henry
Hilda McCloud
Eddie / Elizabeth Johnson
Shelton Brooks
Junior Gardner
Mr. / Mrs. Louis Gardner
Big Gator
Johnny / Maurine Foreman
Winnie / Carolyn Foreman
Melvin Foreman
Melinda Foreman
Samuel / J.W. Foreman
James Odell Foreman
Joyce Eden
Patrick Henry
Nolan / Colbert Smith
Bennie Smith
Willie Johnson
Kenneth Adams
Val Shorter Maxey
Wessie Mae Dobbins
Eddie Bradford, Sr.
Joe Craddock
Walter Jackson
Willie Hudson
Lorenzo Jamison
Gus Hardeman
J.A. Malveaux
Leroy / Ruth Tolliver
Mildred OwenMr. & Mrs. Pom
Roy Coleman

Rose Jackson Bonner
Alice Jones
Pottie / Audrey Green
Katherine Sherwood
Sam Woods
Tim Alexander
Bobbie Yell Rhem
Lucille Cole
Arthur Hawkins
Safornia Terrell
Commodore Sanford
Johnny Henderson
Melvin / Nettie Stephens
Claudette Caldwell Gauthier
Thelma Flemons
Mattie Cole
Helean Dickerson
Theodore / Anita Craddock
Roy Jackson
Lawyer Bluitt
Estelle Carr
Jasper / Dorothy Victoria
Doris Spikes Woodland

Curtis Lee Jones, Sr.
Beatrice Claybon
Evelyn Marie Lewis
Daisy Swan Buster
Clarence "Pee Wee" Swan
Williams W. Clark
Geraldine Pointer Sayler
Shirley Pointer Wilredge
William "Donnie" Wilredge
Carol Henry Johnson
Diane Dickey
Charles Earl Henry
Kenneth / Steve Henry
Louise Woodkins
Ronnie / Lois / Georgia Johnson
Phillip "Tootsie" Meyer
Pauline Williams
Sherman Montgomery
Mary Lee Moses
Wessie Mae Dobbins
Jeffrey / Louise Avie
A.J. / Ruth Hood
Calvin Vincent (Principal)

The "Rec" Sanders Center

It was no secret that there was a need for a recreational facility in the African American community of Texas City. To meet this need, an existing building was donated and had to be moved from a football field. This building promptly and proudly became known as "The Rec." Later, plans and promises to erect a new building were made and fulfilled. This new facility was named in memory of George Sanders. Mr. Sanders not only named the Booker T. Washington School but was also the first principal. The new recreation facility that emerged to take the place of "The Rec" became well known, and most respected, as the "Sanders Center." It remained there until the City of Texas City's reconstruction plans in 2011. The Sanders Center was a staple of the community's outings and events. The many wonderful memories that were made there were captured and embedded in the hearts of the community.

The Swimming Pool

Restrictions prevented the African Americans of Texas City from partaking in recreational activities beyond Texas Ave. As such, a designated recreation area was created for the black neighborhoods. A swimming pool was eventually built in this recreation area. The swimming pool was well received and appreciated. It gave members of the community with a real talent for swimming and diving a chance to excel, and to “show out.” The pool had a special section for toddlers and other young children to ensure their safety. For many children, and young adults, this pool was a comfortable environment in which they learned to swim. The pool was so important to so many of the Booker T. Washington High School students that they began to host school reunions there.

The Projects

"The Projects" referred to the neighborhood surrounding the old Sanders Center. Due to many restrictions, housing for the black people of Texas City had many limitations. People were not content to live and let live during this era. Black people did not have the privilege of moving freely to any area they desired. The Housing Projects became the answer to compensate for this reality. The Housing Authority built apartments for families with low incomes. The projects became a city within a city, a totally black facility. It gave single mothers and parents a chance to live, and, proceeding with caution, a way to survive in a segregated world. Over time, the projects, as a community, earned respect in the City of Texas City.

Marcia Richards Ellison

As I Lived It From *Whence I Came*

Those of us directly affected by the effects of the Diaspora are more alike than we may realize. While we have superficial differences of language, geography, clothes, and varying shades of melanin, we share a common bond. This bond is shaped in seared memory of the Motherland regardless of which coast our ancestors started from and which port we ended up.

We also share what Chimamanda Ngozi Adichie often calls "the single story." Adichie is a Nigerian born novelist, scholar, and storyteller who speaks about the dangers of the single story. When a story about and people is one-sided, the downside is that it robs people on one end of the spectrum of their voice. The single story emphasizes how we are no different rather than how we have similarities. The danger of the single story is that it has no balance.

Those of us who are Black and whose ancestors were born and grew up in America grew up hearing a single story, until a few short decades ago. This story gave little acknowledgement to our trials, our triumphs, and gave no notice to our culture. What we learned about us came from us. In the case of my hometown, Texas City, Texas, that was enough.

Texas City, Texas is a town that is not so different from thousands of other American cities and towns. Black residents of Texas City learned how to turn their trials into triumphs. Like many others in my hometown, I was born in Galveston, Texas but Texas City was my hometown. As I was growing up, I always was considered an atypical place. Born just before the Supreme Court ruling in Brown v. Board of Education struck down segregation in schools, my insulated and segregated upbringing in Texas City provided all that I needed. I felt part of a village of neighbors and teachers who nurtured me, encouraged me and who provided me a safe space to learn and grow.

My teachers at Booker T. Washington School were not boxed in by rigid lesson plans, so Black History was incorporated into almost every subject that I attended. I was doubly fortunate because many of my friends and lunch buddies were our own teachers who were schoolteachers and/or coaches at Booker T. Washington School: Iverson Godfrey, Dr. Dorothy House Godfrey, Sarah Jane Godfrey Giles, Joseph Godfrey Jackson. My uncle Woodrow Wesley Godfrey (who earned multiple degrees from Prairie View A&M) taught at Booker T. Washington School. Other teachers such as William Goff, Billie Johnson, Mrs. Hilda Thomas, T. Fancer, James A. Wilson, Lois Davenport, Rosa Ealbeck, Ethel B. Vincent, Gabriellea Scott, and Billie F. Johnson were all instrumental in shaping young minds. Some were my neighbors. Some were my church friends. Some were individuals.

I could therefore not escape the hereditary desire to learn all I could. Church was also an important component of learning. My church was one of the many churches what would now be called pre-K at my church home - Greater Barbours Chapel Baptist Church. I must have been about three years old when I began to attend Vacation Bible School at Greater Barbours Chapel Baptist Church. I must have been about three years old when I began to attend Vacation Bible School at Greater Barbours Chapel. I was also an assistant to the Church Secretary (Mrs. Bessie Adams), so I could see what went on behind the church doors even when I was not in the main room. She taught me how to type and how to file church documents.

All of these were building blocks in shaping my understanding of what "true North" was. The elders of the church were mentors and role models: Rev. Samuel Howard, Mr. Robert Highbarger, Mrs. Lucille Artis. Mrs. Ollie Coleman. Rev. Andrew Giles.

My mother graduated from the Galveston Business Institute (Salutatorian of her class) and was a whiz at typing and dictation. She was therefore the secretary of many churches, schools, and civic organizations. More often than not, I was at many of these meetings.

My father-Clarence Godfrey- was an equally important component in the shaping of my world view. I can remember at age of six or seven always being very excited as I rode with him to the local newsstand on Texas Ave to get the latest copy of Jet or Ebony or the Pittsburgh Courier. He loved history and he loved knowing about what was happening in the world.

My father also loved sports. While he was not formally and academically trained as his brothers and sisters, he coached basketball in the Booker T. Washington gym and mentored young men in the neighborhood. He had great respect for learning, and he was the one who had conversations with my teachers at the PTA conferences. A grade of “C” was never accepted or acceptable.

At some point both my mother and my father were members of an organization called the Community Development Council. There were beginning to be rumblings nationwide about equality and freedom and integration and the mood in my village was in line with that reality. By necessity we already had a strong entrepreneurial spirit. Many men and women in my community already had an independent methodology. Integration, then, would only enhance what we already were already doing.

Johnnie Henderson developed an early interest in the power of unions. He eventually worked his way up the union ladder and was on a first name basis with many national union and political leaders.

Ceary Johnson was a local businessman who got more than a few Texas City residents out of tight spots. George Eden was a tough cop who practiced his own version of scared straight. He most likely kept more than a few young men from criminal records.

Clara Washington was the owner of a local neighborhood corner store. She never left her store but was aware of everything that happened in the neighborhood. Her store was a safe haven for young kids to shop in safety.

Ella Mae Henry had no children, but she took an interest in several young ladies in the neighborhood and attempted to teach us how to sew, and knit, and learn cute little inexpensive do-it-yourself projects. We named her club, The Friendly Arts Club, and gathered at her house. Many of us learned how to do tasks that have stayed with us to this day.

I became friends with Mrs. "Sugar" Johnson in my early 20's. We had great woman-to-woman conversations. She was so pleased that I expressed a continued interest in sewing that she gave me a sewing machine when I went off to college.

Or Mrs. Lucille Artis, who guided us in the church Baptist Young People's Training Union (BYPU). As integration loomed large on the horizon, she instructed us on how to conduct ourselves as young men and women when we shopped in the downtown stores.

My single story, then, is a positive one. What was meant to exclude provided my community with the tools needed to teach us survival skills. And we survived in both big and little ways. We became local politicians and educators and entertainers and entrepreneurs and men and women of God and lots of "working everyday people. So, our community will be alright, and our single story is one that says we were and always will be survivors.

Mary Godfrey, B.A., M.A., PhD
MGOD and Associates

Wednesday's Children

To all the survivors of the Texas City Disaster
50 Anniversary, April 16, 1997

There was not a war that Wednesday morning, but they say after a thunder sound an eerie mushroom of thick gray-black smoke went high into the sky. It was not wartime, but missiles and debris split the air. No, it was not wartime, but like the aftermath of a great battle, the land was left blood-soaked, burned and charred, death and destruction lay about.

But rising up from these charred ruins catastrophic loss of lives, limbs, and property; marching forward relentlessly across fifty years, they moved. These are Wednesday's Children. Smoldering ember, horrid memories, simmering just below the surface, in their mind to be recalled, flesh of ghastly light that dreaded Wednesday morning, when the Grand Camp Exploded.

With the great blast, a young, unsuspecting town was catapulted to harsh maturity. Help came quickly from far and near to lend a hand. Some outsiders would come. "But where is the little city called 'Texas City'" and reply would come, "why it's by the bay down there, you know where, where they had the great explosion in 47." "But I hear through shredded tears, they've rebuilt over the years. Yes, all of Wednesday's children, like noted phoenix, with their collective wings of faith, hope, courage, resolve, and hard work, they've risen from the ashes and the rubble to soar to new heights.

Indeed, these are Wednesday's children, a testament of the will of a believing people.
Hazel Jones

Killed 1947 Disaster

Mason Cunningham – Joyce Naborne's Father
Harrison Aldridge – H.T. Aldridge's Father
Ennis Norris, Sr. – Ellen Norris

Booker T. Washington Classmates killed in the Texas City Disaster of 1947

Charles Davis
Harold Lloyd Bradford
Melvin "Boncie" Smith
W.C. Coleman
Stellie Barkey
Saul Young
Eddie Lee Hogan

Policemen

In Order:
Wil Gilbert
Louis Gardner
Big Isaac
Red Washington
Willie Cole
Eddie Jennings
Fred Monroe
Peter Bell
George Eden

Killed in Wars

Bubba Jennings – WWII – 1940's 9th Street South
Lucious La Strape – WWII – 1940's 3rd Street South
Lawrence Williams – Veteran 1960's 1st Avenue South
Rufus Hood – Veteran (KIA) 1960's 2nd Avenue South

Businesses of Yesteryear

Kings Grocery
Mrs. Clara's Stand
Gertrude' Beauty Salon
Josie Wade Beauty Shop
Tucker's Cab/Garage
Walter Beasley's Shine Stand
Little City's Shine Stand
Perkin's Bar-B-Que Place
Jay's Inn
Gary's Café/Grocery
Wise Adam's Barber Shop
Johnny Martin's Tavern
Durgeon
Beamer's Café/Hotel
Malveaux's Barber Shop
Bronco's Place

Honey Dripper Café
Big Babe Mechanic Shop
Rollin Café/Hotel
Willie Green's Café
Tommie Grimes Café
Williams Grocery
Jamison Place
Lee Roy/Ruth Toliver's Eating Place
Mrs. Katie's Corner Store
Mrs. Moore's Café/Store
Big Wheel's Place
Joe Louis Gambling Shack
Carey's Pool Hall
Blue Whale Café
Mainland Janitorial Services
Clara Butler's Beauty Shop
Mrs. Hunter's Store
Craddock Hamburger Store
James William Photography
Field's Funeral House
Trampline
Pop's Shine Stand

Early Pioneers

Engulfed in this shrine are more than 50 families that were early settlers and lived in Texas City from 1911 to 2004. The list can never be completed.

Professor George Sanders' Family
Johnny & Fannie Martin
Cearky Johnson
Booker Johnson
Jim / Ethel Brooks
Conquest Simpson (Charles Brown's Grandfather)
Dee, Alyl Ethel Simpson
Pernell Wafers
Rev. F.D. Evans
Ivory Doris
Mr. & Mrs. Bates
Wade Allen (the only Black person working up town/Board of Trust)
Lulu Allen
Matt Parker Cole (1918)
Ned Ellison (1924)
Ruby Ellison
John Maria Hunter
Pink Williams
James Scott Family
Johnny Harden Family
Wise Adams Family
W.L. Craddock Family
Mr. & Mrs. Theodora/Anita Craddock
Leon Williams Family
Tom Eduards Family

Sam Woods Family
Tom / Marie Family
The Commuse Family
Mr. & Mrs. Paul / Mary Gordon
Earl King Sr. Family
John Franklin
Rev. R. Mayes, Sr. & Family
Mr. & Mrs. Arthur Miles
Edna / Eddis Hogan
Gertude Hogan
Russel Rice Family
Gus Hardeman
Louis Parker Family
Arthur / Viola Miles
Eva Wilson
Lillie Steel
John Marie Hunter
Lonnie McClure Clure
Will Gilbert
Anna Wycoff
Rev. P.D. Wisby, Sr.
The Womacks
Comfront Lee
Bessie Adams
Phillip / Marie Spillan (1975)
Mr. & Mrs. Jim / Mary Mack
Mrs. Bill
Monk Roland
Joe Weaver
Joe Mitchell
Gilbert Johnson
Frank / Geadis Evans
Katie Monroe

Ethel / Marie Monroe
Willis Martin Family
Rev. Joe McCloud Family
Mr. & Mrs. C.B. Scales
Lacy / Beatrice James & Family
Mildred Owens / L.C Owens
Howard Rollins, Sr.
Omie Womack
Clarence Calwell Family
Tolliver Family
The Rays Family
The McCall Family
Osha Randle Family
Ischa Family
Gilbert / Evelina Wilredge (Brooks)
Edward Williams Family
Lucille / Willie Cole
Eastryern / Lightfoot Family
The Tisdom Family
Jamees / Eva Lee
Namomi Price Family
The Butler Family
The Brooks Family
The Kimble Family
Pete Jackson
John / Cenia Anderson
Chris Smith
Joe / Sarah Howard
Lucille Johnson Artis
Rev. J.H Scott (BCC)
Rev. Ruben (FBC)
Mr. & Mrs. William Fuller

(GMC)
Johnny / Mable Griffin
Oliver / Elnora Swan (1928)
Preston 'Blue' Spry (1926)
Mary Tillman
(Bell Toner Community)
Harry / Hazel Williams, Sr.

Prairie View A&M University

Prairie View A&M University Interscholastic League Coaches Association School/Hall of Famers from Booker T. Washington High School.

Clarence Caldwell 2012
Griggs Owens Jr 2012
Martha Payne Darden 2015
Mercie D. Prevost 2017
Otis Pointer Sr 2015
Lynn Ray Ellison 2015
Charles "Mack" Phillips 2019

Booker T. Washington Final Roll Call

A.D Beaves
Agnes Ricks
Albert Dixon
Alfred Brown
Alfred Dennis
Alfred Williams
Alice Faye Cleveland
Allen Morris
Alma Dean Young
Alzina Rice
Annie Mae Simpson
Annie Ruth McAfee
Anthony McCloud
Archie Scott
Arletha Baker Cofield
Armer Lee Kimble
Arthur Jean Woods
Audrey Rice Black

Duke Walker
Dwight Wilredege
Earl "Poochie" Payne
Earl Leon King
Earline King
Early Carpenter
Earnest Bogan, Jr.
Earnest Harper
Earnest Parker
Earnestine Boston
Earnstine McDaniel
Eddie Johnson Sr.
Eddie Lee Hogan
Eddie V. Carter

Edward Carter
Elizabeth Young
Ella Ruth Swan
Eloise Smith Goldman
Emmit Parker

Jackie Rice
Jacqueline Davison
Jamer Roberson
James Adams, Sr.
James Cooper
James Lee Adams, Jr.
Jammy Lee Ray
Jerome Evans
Jerry "Put" Scales
Jerry Simpson
Jesse McFarland
Jessie "O" Brien
Jessie W. Scott
Jet Johnson
Jo Ann Johnson
Joe Craddock
Joe McCloud
John Maseh
Johnny Mae Morris

Oral Lee Carter
Otha Green, Jr.
Pearlie Mae Jones Craddock
Phillip Meyes
Pothenie Lynch
Quincy Moses
Quinnie Lee Mosely
Ralph Williams

Randolph Lynch
Randolph Scott
Ray Duhon
Raynell Barbin
Richard Felder, Jr
Richard Jones
Rita Guss
Rita Johnson
Robbie Caldwell
Robbie Caldwell Campbell
Robbie Mae Johnson
Barbara Holland
Beauty B Collins
Bennie Creamer
Bernadette Walker
Bernice Bean
Bertha Lee Young
Bessie Mae Williams
Betty Hill
Betty Reed Bennett
Betty Thompson
Betty Tryals
Billie Waters
Bobbie Griffin
Bobbie Smith
Bobbie Young
Brenda Jackson
Brenda Randall
Bruce Ellison
Bubba Creamer
Calvin Comier, Sr.
Calvin Comier, Jr.
Calvin Vincent

Carl Davis
Carl Tryals
Carol Ann Tolliver
Carolyn Foreman
Carolyn Warren Sherwood
Cecil Caldwell
Cecil Henderson
Charles "Nutbaby" Johnson
Charles Granger
Charles Sawyer
Charlie Harris
Charlie Jackson
Chris Young
Emmitt Parker
Eric Houston
Ernest Lee Williams
Ervin Miles (Bro. Miles)
Estella Blaylock
Estella Scott
Ethel Scott McFarland
Ethel Vincent
Eura V. Shorter
Evelyn "Pete" Williams
Evelyn Hogan Burns
Evelyn McClure
Fannie Tootie Jamerson
Faye Evans Woodard
Flora Sanford
Floyd Marshall
Ford Marie Lester
Frank Johnson
Freddie Fletcher
Freddie Washington, Sr.
Freddie Washington, Jr.
Gabriel Lena Scott
Gail Ellison Dottin
George "Mountain" Long
George Ray
George Ray
Girmon V. Ferris
Gladys Caldwell
Gloria Jean Hardy
Gloria Johnson
Gloria Rhem Parker
Gloria Rockmore
Gloria T. Armstrong
Grady Berry, Jr.
Hambone Dugard
Johnny Mae Morris
Johnny Tryals, Sr.
Johnny Tryals, Jr.
Johnny Wright (Bo Dog)
Josephine Crudup
Joyce Marie Mayes
Joyce Montgomery
Joyce Robinson
Julius Butler Brigley
Justene Woodkins Williams
Katherine Nelson
Kathryn Walker
Kenneth Adams
Kenneth Henry
Kenneth Jones
L.J. James
Larry Scott
Lavern Cofield Rice

Lawrence Wortham
Lee Otis Burnett
Lee Roy Hardy, Sr.
Lee Roy Hardy, Jr.
Leo Lynch
Leroy Gary, Sr.
Leroy Gary, Jr.
Leroy Hudson
Lewis Adams
Lillie Alexis Mitchell
Linda Shaw
Lively Walker, Sr.
Lloyd Burke Stevens
Lloyd Francis
Lloyd Richards
Loris Davenport
Louis Parker
Robert Macon
Robert Corfield
Robert Flint
Robert Gordon
Robert Griffin
Robert Griffin, Jr.
Robert James
Robert Jones
Robert Lee Campbell
Robert Phoenix
Robert Rice
Robert Ware
Robert Williams
Roger Barrett
Ronnie McClinton
Ronnie Rhem
Rosa Eelbeck
Rose Swan
Rosie Gillis
Roy Henry Tolliver
Roy Swan
Russell Rice
Sadie Mayes
Sammy Young
Sandra Ann Amey
Saul Young
Selaine Rollins
Sherrril Lee Ellison
Shirley Victoria Mann
Sonny Steven
Sonny Young
Stella Wilredege
Stellie Barkey
Thomas Carter, Jr.
Thomas Swan, Jr.
Charlie Jackson
Chris Young
Clarence Gordon, Jr.
Classie Mae Green
Cleo Young
Cleveland Gay
Cleveland Jones
Cliff Jones, Sr.
Clifford Aaron
Cozy Brown
Darcy M. Griffin
Delaine Marie Phillips
Delores Sneed
Dimple Ray Lewis

Dit Simpson
Donnie Wildridge
Doris Collins
Doris Jean Lynn
Doris Sue Wildredge
Dorothy Crudip
Dorothy Sanford
Douglas Watson
Hambone Dugard
Harold Adams
Harold Lloyd Bradford
Harvey D. Tryals
Hattie Felder
Hazel Caldwell
Hazel Williams
Helen W. Watkins
Henderson Johnson
Henry "Plute" Williams
Henry Lee Jackson
Herbert Swan
Herman Felder
Herman Newsome
Homer Lee Rollins, Jr.
Hosey Jefferson
Howard Rollins, Jr.
Inez Rick Ferguson
Irene Kimble
Iverson Godfrey, Jr.
J.B. Burnett
J.W. Foreman
Louis Parker
Mae "Nip" Jeanette Green
Margaret Bradford
Marie Allen
Marvin Bridges
Mary Caldwell
Mary Linda Booker
Mattie Moore
Mattie Pearl Thomas
MeAnn Dugard Adams
Melba Cunningham Hall
Melvin Bunce Smith
Melvin Foreman
Mercille Sherwood
Merdis McClinton
Michael Evans
Milton Evans
Myrtle Hood
Nathan Batiste
Nathaniel Myers
Norma Garrett
Octavia Swan
Thomas Swan, Sr.
Tommy Joe Brooks
Travis Scott
Vera Smith
Vilanthea Waddy Ricks
Virdie Crudip
Vivian King
W.C. Coleman
Wayne Wade
Wendel Duhon
Willa Bonner
Willetta Mayes
William Hayes
William Patin

Williams Carr
Willie D. Wright
Willie Lee Dixon
Willie Lloyd, Jr.
Willie Mae Dugard
Wilmer Jones
Winford Bonner
Yotoshia Wisley Barker

Black American Churches Established North of Texas Avenue

Mount Zion Baptist Church
College View Church of Christ
Little Zion Baptist Church
Faith Mission Church of Prayer
House of Prayer
Truc Worship Baptist Church
Grace and Mercy Church

The Faces of Southside

The Faces of Southside

The Faces of Southside

The Faces of Southside

The Faces of Southside

Southside's Favorite Son

Joe "Pogo Joe" Caldwell

High School All-American 1960 – College All-American 1960-1964 • United States Olympic Team gold medal Winner 1964 • All NBA Rookie of the Year, First Round Pick 1965 • Best Defensive Player in NBA 1966-1967, 1968-1969, Highest Season scorer points (23.5)

and the list goes on ...

Lineage Beyond Place

The South Community's legacy did not remain contained within its original ten-block footprint. As families dispersed, so too did the values cultivated along First Avenue South—discipline, faith, resilience, and expectation. In some cases, that legacy became visible on national and international stages. The lives of Joe *Pogo Joe* Caldwell and Charles Brown illustrate how the South Community's influence traveled outward, carried not as memory alone but as lived practice.

Joe *Pogo Joe* Caldwell
Southside's Favorite Son

Joe "Pogo Joe" Caldwell rose from the heart of South Phoenix to become one of the most electrifying athletes of his generation. Born in 1941 and raised in the tight-knit Southside community, Caldwell carried the pride of his neighborhood everywhere he went. His nickname, "Pogo," came honestly—he seemed to spring off the hardwood with a force and grace that defied physics, a player who could hang in the air long enough to make crowds gasp.

Caldwell's talent announced itself early. By 1960 he was a High School All-American, a hometown hero whose name traveled far beyond the desert. At Arizona State University, he became a College All-American (1960–1964), anchoring one of the most dynamic teams in the school's history. His explosive athleticism earned him a place on the 1964 U.S. Olympic basketball team, where he helped bring home a gold medal from Tokyo—an achievement that forever linked South Phoenix to the world stage.

In 1965, Caldwell entered the NBA as a first-round draft pick for the Detroit Pistons, stepping onto the professional stage with the same explosive energy that had defined his college career. He made an immediate impact, earning NBA All-Rookie honors and establishing himself as one of the league's most relentless defenders. His instincts, speed, and vertical made him a problem for anyone who tried to score, and it was not long before he was recognized as one of the best defensive players in the game. His scoring ability peaked with a season average of 23.5 points, showcasing a versatility that made him dangerous on both ends of the court. Later, in the ABA, he became one of the rare athletes to be an All-Star in both leagues, a testament to his longevity and impact.

But beyond the stats and accolades, Joe Caldwell remained what Southside always claimed him to be, their favorite son. He carried his community with him into every arena, every locker room, every headline. His story is not just about basketball; it's about possibility. It's about a young man from South Phoenix who jumped higher, ran faster, and dreamed bigger than anyone expected, and in doing so, lifted an entire neighborhood with him.

Charles Brown was a frequent visitor to the Frank Jr. and Ollie Bell house, where he entertained the neighborhood playing on Ollie's piano.

Charles Brown

Before the world knew his name, before the West Coast blues carried his voice into nightclubs and jukeboxes across America, Charles Brown was simply a quiet, observant boy growing up along the Gulf Coast, born in Texas City, Texas, on September 13, 1922, in a world still shaped by the rhythms of the port, the refinery lights, and the slow, humid cadence of coastal life. His earliest memories were not of fame or applause but of the steady insistence of his grandmother, Swanee Simpson, who believed that discipline, education, and music were the keys that could open any door for a Black child in the Jim Crow South.

His mother died shortly after his birth, and so Texas City became both cradle and compass. The Simpson household was strict but loving, a place where expectations were high, and idleness had no room to grow.

Swanee insisted that Charles learn the piano—not as a hobby, but as a language. She believed music could shape a boy's character, sharpen his mind, and give him a way to speak in a world that often refused to listen. Under her watchful eye, Charles practiced scales until his fingers learned to glide, not strike. He absorbed the hymns of Barbour's Chapel Baptist Church, where he first played publicly, and where the congregation recognized something in him, an emotional clarity, a softness, a way of making the piano feel like a confession.

Texas City in the 1920s and 1930s was a place of contradictions: industry and coastline, segregation and community, hardship and resilience. Charles grew up watching men leave home before dawn to work the docks or the refineries, their clothes carrying the smell of oil and saltwater. He saw women hold families together with quiet strength. He learned early that survival required both grit and grace. Those lessons would later seep into his music, the slow burn of his blues, the tenderness in his voice, the unhurried phrasing that felt like a man telling the truth without raising it above a whisper.

By the time he reached adolescence, Charles had outgrown the musical boundaries of Texas City. He was drawn to the broader world of sound—jazz, classical, and the emerging blues styles drifting across the Gulf from New Orleans. His talent was undeniable, but so was his intellect. He graduated from Central High School in Galveston in 1939 and pursued a degree in chemistry at Prairie View A&M, a path that reflected both his academic discipline and the practical realities of Black life in the South. Music was his gift, but education was his armor.

Even as he worked as a chemistry teacher, a mustard gas worker during World War II, and later as an apprentice electrician, the piano remained his truest companion. The world was shifting, and Charles felt the pull of something larger than Texas City—an invitation to step into the life he had been preparing for since childhood. In 1943, he left Texas for Los Angeles, carrying with him the quiet confidence of a man who knew exactly who he was.

Los Angeles was a different universe, fast, bright, and alive with possibility. But Charles did not chase the noise. He brought with him the Texas City softness, the Gulf Coast patience, the church-trained restraint. When he joined Johnny Moore's Three Blazers, his voice and piano style immediately set him apart. Where other blues singers shouted their pain, Charles delivered his like a confession, intimate, deliberate, and devastatingly honest. His breakout hit, *Drifting Blues*, was not just a song; it was a new emotional vocabulary. It stayed on the Billboard R&B chart for six months and became a blueprint for the West Coast blues sound.

Through the late 1940s and early 1950s, Charles Brown became a quiet giant of American music. His hits, *Trouble Blues, Black Night,* and *Hard Times,* were not loud declarations but slow, simmering truths. His influence shaped artists like Ray Charles, Floyd Dixon, and Ivory Joe Hunter, all of whom borrowed from the emotional restraint and melodic clarity he perfected.

Yet no matter how far he traveled, Texas City remained the root system beneath his success. The discipline of his grandparents, the church that first trusted his hands on the piano, the Gulf Coast air that taught him to move at his own pace, all of it lived inside his music. His sound was not born in Los Angeles; it was born in a small Texas town where a boy learned that softness could be a form of strength.

Charles Brown died on January 21, 1999, in Oakland, California, but his legacy continues to ripple across American music. He is a member of the Rock and Roll Hall of Fame, a recipient of the W.C. Handy Award, and one of the architects of modern rhythm and blues. But before all of that, he was a Texas City son, a child shaped by the Gulf, by family, by faith, and by the quiet determination that would one day make him a legend.

His story is not just the story of a musician. It is the story of a boy who learned to turn discipline into elegance, hardship into melody, and a Texas City upbringing into a sound that would change American music forever.

First Baptist Church History

The First Baptist Church was organized in 1914. A meeting was called by the late Rev. J. S. Bell with a consecrated few, five men and two women: the late Bro. Joe Lightfoot, Bro. Cleveland Burton, Bro. W. W. Love, Bro. Lee Dowels, Sis. Lela Beardshard and Sis. Clara Thornton. The first worship service was held in an old business house near Sixth Street. Later, in 1915, one lot was purchased at the present location, 819 First Avenue South (now known as M. L. King Jr. Ave.). A small building was constructed in 1916 under the pastorate of Rev. D. A. Jones. In July 1916, a new church was under construction and completed in the spring of 1917. Electric lights were installed in 1919.

In 1919, Rev. D. A. Jones was called to another church. He was followed by eleven other pastors, the last of whom was the Rev. L. G. Rubin. For a while, the church had no pastor, although there was a minister to preach every Sunday. The Rev. Frank M. Johnson came one of those Sunday mornings, preached, and gave the membership a needed spiritual uplifting. The church gave the late Bro. James H.

Williams (church clerk), permission to invite Rev. Johnson back again. In April 1946, Rev. Johnson was recommended to the congregation by the late Rev. J. F. Sargent and the Rev. F. A. Allen. In the same year, Rev. Johnson accepted the invitation, and the church's present blessing of a faithful pastor began.

One year after Rev. Johnson became pastor, on April 16 and 17, the church building was destroyed in what was known as the "Great Texas City Disaster." The neighboring church, Galilee United Methodist, permitted the membership to hold evening worship services in their church.

Under the pastorate of Rev. Johnson, the church has grown numerically, spiritually and financially. He has been proven to be one of God's spirit-filled servants. A pastor, leader, teacher and a songster. A familiar quote of Pastor Johnson is "To take a little bit of I, and a great part of me, and place them in the hands of God, who made salvation free. If you find the giving part won't do what must be done, then give more like the Father, who gave His only Son."

When remembering the House of God of long ago when Rev. Johnson first came, it was a house to praise God in but there was no carpet on the floor, push-up windows for air with a fan in the hand, gas heaters in the winter, no water fountains and a cooler with ice. There was not even a pool in which to be baptized, but we went down to the bay, and many were baptized there.

In 1957, the parsonage was moved and renovated. It is now located at 718 M. L. King, Jr. Ave. The property was purchased from the George Austin family. The church purchased property on the east side of the church from the McCloud and Pointer families in order to build and provide fenced-in parking. Across the street from the church, property was purchased from the Wisby family. A house is enclosed within the fence of the church, and property was also purchased from the West

Texas City for future use. All of this was accomplished under the pastorate of Rev. Johnson. In November 1957, the cornerstone was laid by Pride of Texas City Lodge #193 F&A Masons. June 1, 1958, with Rev. Johnson leading, we marched into the house that was dedicated to God: The First Baptist Church. On June 12, 1968, the mortgage was burned in ceremony.

Fifteen ministers have confessed their calling to the Gospel under Pastor Johnson, five have been ordained for Pastorate.

Additions have been made to the church since 1958, such as a new Fellowship Hall, a picture room, a well-equipped kitchen, beautiful windows, outdoor carpets, three church vans, and guard rails for seniors.

Congratulations is due to Pastor F. M. Johnson for fifty years of full leadership.

The First Baptist Church Family
Ethel M. Brown, Church Historian
Raymond C. Woodkins, Clerk
Rev. F. M. Johnson, Pastor

Mt. Paran Missionary Baptist Church

The Mt. Paran Missionary Baptist Church was organized on March 9, 1961, in the dining room of Booker T. Washington School in Texas City, Texas. The following ministers were present: Rev. Wiley Dunn, Rev. F. M. Johnson, Rev. Forest Chambers, Rev. Herman Hensley, Rev. E. J. Johnson and Rev. E. J. Johnson of Houston, Texas. The history of the church becomes etched back several years, for it was then that God had the organization of a church in the Texas City area in the mind of the man of God who was to become our pastor, the Rev. E. J. Johnson. At that time, moved by the spirit of God, Pastor Johnson began conducting Sunday School classes for, indeed, he was moved to attend the regular Sunday School morning classes, and God blessed his efforts. It had meaning. On March 9th, that meeting was conducted by Rev. Wiley L. Dunn, and Rev. E. J. Johnson spoke on the subject, "A Christians Endeavor: Manual for the delivery of a Missionary Message." Rev. E. J. Johnson spoke, and a motion was made by Dr. Lucius Trayls to organize the Texas City area. The motion was seconded by Rev. Arthur Johnson. Six members were received that night, and a motion was made to call the church, "Mt. Paran Missionary Baptist Church".

Sis Bobbie Jean Garrett was appointed secretary. Bro. Lucius Tryals was appointed treasurer, and Rev. E. J. Johnson was elected unanimously to become the first Pastor of Mt. Paran Missionary Baptist Church. The congregation immediately set about the task of building a church in which to worship. Six months later, on the 2nd Sunday in August 1961, the congregation marched into their new edifice at 102 Texas Avenue. Six years later, the church was remodeled.

The pastor had the foresight to make preparation for the future. With hard work and blessings from God, the church membership began to grow and with the growth of the membership, it was necessary to expand and build a new church.

After obtaining a permit to build the church on July 8, 1974, at 1649-56 Street North, Rev. Johnson began the task of constructing the new building. Three months later, in October, the partially constructed structure collapsed. The walls came tumbling down!

This, however, did not stop the vision of Pastor Johnson. After a sleepless night, Pastor Johnson and others vowed to start again and continue the task that God had given. Their faith was being tested, and Pastor Johnson, with unwavering faith, was able to cross paths with someone sent by God.

The building was in ruins, and after viewing the site, it was brought back to life by the late Mr. John Godard. Mr. Godard funded the church financially, as well as supplying the equipment and laborers.

Pastor Johnson was truly grateful to God for sending Mr. Godard and allowing him to be the major financial contributor that was needed to help revive the reconstruction of the church.

On the 3rd Sunday in June 1976, the Lord blessed Mt. Paran again to move into the new location, 19 Sixth Street North. The Cornerstone was installed at the church free of charge by Osbe Sherwood. Entrance Day Service was officiated by Rev. H. A. Ratcliff, Jr.

On July 30, 1995, the Lord blessed the Mt. Paran Family with the installation of Rev. Dr. W. W. Jackson, Jr. as pastor and Mt. Paran became members of the Lincoln District Missionary Baptist Association of Texas in which Rev. Jackson later became the Moderator.

On April 14, 1996, the cafeteria was dedicated as the Rev. J. Johnson Fellowship Hall. On September 7, 1997, a ribbon-cutting ceremony was held for a Youth Church in the adjacent building to the church. In 1998 and 2000, Mt. Paran was blessed with the acquisition of additional property directly in front of the church and the property was paved and turned into a beautiful parking lot.

God blessed the late Rev. Dr. W. W. Jackson, Jr. to serve over 20 years. Through God's guidance and the leadership and faith of Pastor Jackson, Mt. Paran continued onward and upward, proclaiming the word of God.

On October 5, 2015, Rev. Q. C. Wallace was elected as the Pastor of Mt. Paran Missionary Baptist Church. He served as pastor until October 24, 2016. Through God's guidance and the leadership and faith of Pastor Wallace, Mt. Paran continued onward and upward, proclaiming the word of God.

On October 7, 2018, Rev. Reginald C. Rose II was elected as Pastor by the congregation. Rev. Rose was officially installed as Pastor of Mt. Paran on February 17, 2019.

Through God's guidance and vision and faith of Pastor Rose, Mt. Paran will continue onward and upward, proclaiming the word of God. Mt. Paran's motto is Connect, Grow & Serve, Connecting people to Christ one relationship at a time.

Mt. Paran welcomes your prayers as they continue to do the Lord's will and follow the vision of Rev. Reginald C. Rose II. Mt. Paran Missionary Baptist Church, "the Connecting Church," will continue to stand boldly on the word of the Lord and march onward with our heavenly father as our beacon light.

Greater Macedonia Baptist Church

"In September of 1996, Rev. Robert E. Maxey became Pastor of Greater Macedonia Baptist Church. Under his leadership, the church has grown in membership and financially.

The church purchased property in 1997 and proceeded to plan and implement the building of a new edifice. Officers were: Deacon Alfred Duhon, Chairman of the Deacon Board. Deacons: Johnny Owens and Sammie Ward. On trail Deacons were Brothers Leroy Sherwood, Lamar Sherwood, Charles Williams, Lawrence McDaniel, and Marvin White. The Assistant Pastor was Rev. Terrance Bell. The Associate Minister was Rev. William Archie. Brother Sidney Scott was President of the Brotherhood, and Deacon Johnny Owens was President of the Male Chorus."

"Deacon Alfred Duhon, Superintendent of Sunday School, Sister Adell Ward, Secretary of Sunday School, Sister Rose Gladney, Youth Sunday School Teacher and Vice President of Mission #2, Sister Tammie Davis, Assistant Teacher. Mission #2, Sister Delores Bell, President, Sister Murcile Sherwood, Secretary, and Sister Barbera Bogan, Treasurer. Mission #1, Sister Hansie Spiller, President; Sister Tammie Davis, Secretary; Sister Delores Bell, Treasurer. Choir: Sister Sharon Bolton, Secretary, Sister Equilla Lee.

The new edifice was completed in 1999 with Brother Lamar Sherwood as General Contractor. Deacons added to the Deacon board: Leroy Sherwood, Lamar Sherwood, Marvin White, Charles Williams, Lawrence McDaniel, Willie J. Alexander, and Clark Scruggs. Church Historian Dr. Lynn Ray Ellison."

Reverend J.H. Scott

Greater Barbour's Chapel Centennial Moment in History

Reverend James Henry Scott, Sr. was born on September 16, 1910, in Hamburg, Louisiana, to George and Annie Scott. As a young boy, he and his family were members of Mount Olive Baptist Church in Big Cane, Louisiana. At the age of nine, he accepted Christ, was baptized by Reverend Lott, and united with Mount Olive Baptist Church.

As a young man, Scott answered the call to Christian ministry. His seminary studies led him to Baker, Louisiana; Conroe, Texas; and the Mount Gilead Baptist Church School of Ministry in Beaumont, Texas. During this period, he served local churches in numerous capacities. On August 24, 1941, he was licensed to preach, and in 1942, he was ordained at New Hope Missionary Baptist Church in Port Arthur, Texas.

In 1943, Reverend Scott accepted the call to pastor Barbour's Chapel Baptist Church of Texas City, Texas. He became the church's first full-time pastor and served from 1943 to 1959. Under his leadership, the church secured property from the Old Landmark Association; renovated the church structure by elevating the sanctuary; added a balcony; and created provisions for a fellowship hall on the first story. He reorganized the second Sunday as Youth Day, added Usher Board No. 2, organized a junior usher board, expanded the Mission to include several circles, reorganized the Baptist Training Union, established the Deaconess and Trustee boards, organized the Educational Fund department, started Barbour's Chapel Church School, and renamed the church Greater Barbour's Chapel Missionary Baptist Church.

A defining moment of his Texas City pastorate came with the Texas City Disaster of 1947, when two chemical-carrying ships exploded while docked, causing 576 known deaths, thousands of injuries, and widespread destruction. The church was badly damaged, but under Reverend Scott's leadership, members worked tirelessly to repair, redesign, and renovate the building. His ministry emphasized ownership, independence, and educational advancement within the African American community. As an incentive for youth, the Educational Fund was established, beginning in 1952, according to community accounts and formally documented in 1955 when Reverend Scott dedicated his appreciation gift to launch the campaign. The first stipends were issued in September 1955.

In May 1959, guided by prayer and faith, Reverend Scott accepted the call to pastor West Tabernacle Baptist Church in Beaumont, Texas. During his administration, the long-held dream of Reverend Al Price to build a modern church structure was realized. Under Scott's leadership, the church completed its new building, paid off all indebtedness, purchased a parking lot and identification signs, and established its first daycare. A Board of Education and Ministry was also organized, continuing his lifelong emphasis on educational advancement. He served West Tabernacle for 19 years, shepherding the Pear Orchard community with distinction.

Reverend Scott held significant leadership roles beyond the local church. In 1959, he served as Moderator of the Eastern Progressive Missionary Baptist District Association and as Vice President of the Baptist Missionary and Educational Convention of Texas. He was also a member of the Progressive Order of Pilgrims of Houston, a Master Mason of Bishop Grant Lodge No. 72, a member of St. George Consistory No. 101, and a patron of the Eastern Stars.

Reverend James Henry Scott, Sr. served faithfully until the end of his earthly life. He died on July 20, 1978. His legacy endures through the churches he strengthened, the educational pathways he championed, and the communities he transformed.

Lee Giles

To everything there is a season, and for Lee Andrew Giles, that season began on October 14, 1930, in Wharton County, El Campo, Texas, where he was born to the late Rev. Thalzy H. Giles and Mrs. Lela M. Kimble Giles, the second of five children. Raised in a Christian home, he accepted Christ at an early age and united with Grove Hill Baptist Church in the Grove Hill Community, where the late Rev. W. L. Banks baptized him in the river. On December 24, 1946, the Giles family moved to Texas City and united with Greater Barbour's Chapel Baptist Church under the leadership of Pastor J. H. Scott. Lee Andrew began his education in the Grove Hill Community, continued at Powell Point Boarding School in Kendleton, Texas, and completed his studies at Central High School in Galveston, graduating in 1948. He attended college for one year but paused his education so his sister Myrtle could continue hers, a reflection of the generous heart he carried throughout his life. In 1951, he enlisted in the United States Air Force, serving a four-year tour until his honorable discharge.

On December 24, 1954, he married the love of his life, Sarah Jane Godfrey, in a family home in Texas City, with Pastor J. H. Scott officiating. Their union was blessed with two children, Gregory Wane and Andrea Regenia. Lee Andrew was a devoted husband—attentive, patient, and unwavering in his care—serving as chauffeur, caretaker, cook, and constant companion. Together, he and Sarah created a home defined by love, refuge, and service, a place where family and friends found comfort, support, and healing. Even as their health declined, their commitment to caring for others never faltered.

A dedicated Christian man, Lee Andrew loved his church deeply. A member of Greater Barbour's Chapel for 65 years, he served as Financial Secretary for more than 40 years and contributed faithfully as a member of the Trustee Board, Mass Choir, Male Chorus, Men's Sunday School, Brotherhood, the Tutorial Program, and most passionately, as chairperson of the Educational Fund. In 2009, Pastor James E. Brown, Sr. elevated him to Elder of the church. His service extended beyond the church into civic and fraternal life, including memberships in the United Postal Workers Union, Rotary Club, Mainland NAACP, A. Philip Randolph Institute, Texas City/Mainland Chamber of Commerce, Golden Division Chamber of Commerce, the American Legion, and the Southwest Central District Association. He was a 50-plus-year member of the Most Worshipful Prince Hall Grand Lodge of Texas, served as Secretary of Pride of Texas City Lodge #193 before its merger with La Marque Lodge #373 F&AM, and held membership in El Katif Temple #85.

Throughout his working life, Lee Andrew held various jobs, including at the Union Hall and Forest Park East Cemetery, before beginning his career with the United States Postal Service in 1958. He often recalled with pride that he was the first Black man to work at the Texas City Post Office. He later became the first African American Postmaster in La Marque and completed 28 years of service in Houston. In 2011, family and friends established the Lee and Sarah Giles Scholarship Fund to honor their lifelong commitment to education, with the inaugural banquet held in February 2012. Even as his health declined, he remained devoted to his church, last worshipping on October 28 during Family and Friends Day.

On November 3, 2012, after a fruitful life of service, love, and faith, Lee Andrew Giles transitioned from time into eternity. He joined his parents, Rev. T. H. Giles Sr. and Mrs. Lela Kimble Giles; his sister, Gracie Bell Giles Jamerson; his brother, Leon Giles; and many other loved ones. He leaves to cherish his legacy his devoted wife of 57 years, Sarah J. Godfrey Giles; his son, Gregory W. Giles Sr. (Gwendolyn); his daughter, Andrea Regenia Randall (Pastor William L. Randall Jr.); his grandchildren Gregory W. Giles Jr., Jamail Shelton (Latrice), Crystal Randall, Lance Giles, Ashley Randall Scott (DeJuan), and Whitney Randall; five great-grandchildren—Jiah Shelton, LeAndro Giles, Ethan Scott, Sarah Giles, and Brenden Scott; his sister Myrtle Giles Davis (Paul); his brother T. H. "Sonny" Giles Jr.; sister-in-law Ollie Mae Thompson (Charles); and a host of nieces, nephews, extended family, and his beloved Barbour's Chapel Church family.

Jimmie Sherwood

Elder Deacon Jimmie Sherwood lived a life that reflected the scripture, *Let your light shine before men, that they may see your good works, and glorify your Father which is in heaven.* Born on March 29, 1929, on a ranch in Madisonville, Texas, he was one of ten children born to the late Royal and Rebecca Sherwood. He accepted Christ at an early age while attending Midway Baptist Church and received his early education in Madisonville before leaving school to help support his family. After leaving his hometown, he entered the construction industry, working faithfully until his retirement in 1982 from the Laborer's International Union of America. On July 19, 1952, he married the love of his life,

Lois Marie Bates, and together they shared 64 years and eight months of unwavering devotion. Their union was blessed with two daughters whom he cherished deeply.

Those who knew Elder Sherwood understood not only his love for the Lord but also his profound love for animals. Retiring at the age of 53 allowed him to fully embrace his passion for breeding horses and raising cattle. He bred cattle and registered quarter horses through the American Quarter Horse Association, selling and showing them across Texas. His prized horses appeared in the Houston Livestock Show and Rodeo's cutting horse competitions, and he generously allowed young men to show his horses in 4-H and other competitions. Widely respected in the rodeo community, he was recognized as one of the first Black cowboys in Galveston County and honored as Texas City's 1995 Black History Month Outstanding Trail Boss. Though he had no biological sons, he proudly served as a mentor and father figure to many young men.

Elder Sherwood was a quiet, humble man who loved his family deeply. Surrounded by loved ones, he transitioned peacefully, confident in his faith and ready to answer God's call to his Heavenly home. He leaves behind a devoted legacy carried forward by his wife, Lois Marie Sherwood; his daughters, Vanessa G. Riles and Yolanda K. Davis; his "son-in-love," Marcus K. Davis Sr.; grandchildren Kaeona Riles, Candice Davis, Morgan V. Davis, and Marcus K. Davis Jr.; and great-grandchildren Klemile Westbrook, Law'ren, Zo'Riah, Kaydince, and Kynnedi. He is also survived by siblings Osbe Sherwood and Catherine Sherwood McGrue; brothers-in-law Clarence Bates, Timothy Bates, and Alvin Don Bates Sr.; sisters-in-law Ruby Sherwood, Murcille Sherwood, and Glady Bates; seven godchildren; special friends Elder Deacon William Shorter and Deacon Milton Randle; and a host of nieces, nephews, relatives, extended family, church members, and friends.

A devoted servant of Greater Barbour's Chapel Baptist Church, Elder Sherwood will lie in state in the sanctuary from 10:00 a.m. to 12:45 p.m., with the Celebration of Life beginning at 1:00 p.m. on Saturday, March 24, 2018, at 7420 FM 1765 in Texas City. His pastor, Reverend Andrew W. Berry II, will serve as celebrant. Burial will follow at Hayes Grace Memorial Cemetery in Hitchcock, Texas, with the family receiving friends at the church afterward.

William Shorter

Elder Deacon William Shorter's journey of faith and service began long before he became one of the most respected pillars of Greater Barbour's Chapel Baptist Church. In January of 1947, he and his wife, Emeola, moved to Texas City, Texas, where he united with Barbour's Chapel by letter from Sand Ridge Baptist Church in Egypt, Texas. This decision marked the beginning of more than seven decades of unwavering devotion to his church, his pastors, and his community.

Shortly after joining the congregation, he became active in the Senior Choir and the Sunday School Department. His dedication and character were quickly recognized, and he was appointed a Junior Deacon by Rev. James Scott. Over the years, he served faithfully under the leadership of Rev. Reynolds, Rev. L. B. Brown, and Rev. H. A. Ratcliff, offering more than 35 years of continuous service in Christian education and church leadership. Under Rev. Ratcliff, he taught Sunday School, served as Assistant Superintendent, and was later promoted to General Superintendent. He also taught Tuesday night Bible Study, served in the Brotherhood, and was ordained as a Deacon, deepening his commitment to the spiritual growth of the congregation.

As the years progressed, Deacon Shorter's influence only grew. He became known for his passion for studying and teaching God's Word, always prepared with a lesson and always eager to share scripture with anyone he encountered. His wisdom, humility, and steadfast faith made him a trusted mentor and spiritual father to many. In recognition of his lifelong service, he was elevated to the position of Elder, becoming the first Elder in the history of Greater Barbour's Chapel Baptist Church. Even in his later years, he remained active in ministry, serving alongside his daughter Betty and his grandson, continuing to teach and inspire well into his nineties.

Elder Shorter's life of service came to its earthly close in 2023. His Celebration of Life was held at Greater Barbour's Chapel Baptist Church, the very place where he had poured out his gifts for more than seventy years, followed by interment at Grace Memorial Park in Santa Fe, Texas.

Elder Deacon William Shorter leaves behind a legacy defined by faithfulness, humility, and a lifelong commitment to teaching God's Word. His influence continues to live on in the ministries he shaped, the leaders he mentored, and the generations he guided in faith.

Timeline

1913 - Barbour's Est.
December 24, 1946 - Giles Family
January 1947 - The Shorters Arrive
April 1947 - Texas City Disaster
1948 - Facility Renovation
1957 - The Sherwoods
97th Anniversary 2010

Galilee United Methodist Church History

Galilee United Methodist Church was organized on January 1913; its first services were held in a structure on Sixth Street in Texas City, Texas. Later in the year, services were held in a building on First Avenue South between Seventh and Eighth Streets. The church purchased a lot on the corner of First Avenue and Ninth Street, and later exchanged that lot for a lot on Second Avenue at Eighth Street. A building was erected on this property during the tenure of Reverend Josey.

The building was destroyed by fire in 1917 during the pastorate of Reverend D. A. Runnels; Galilee was without a pastor for four years.

Reverend Edgar Thomas was assigned to the church during the 1922 Conference year. A small church was built and was destroyed during a storm in 1932. The church then acquired the property on the corner of First Avenue South and Seventh Street. The church was rebuilt under the pastorate of Reverend L.A. Daniels, who was pastor to Galilee, along with a church in Dickinson.

In 1942, Reverend James Perryman was assigned as pastor with an approximate membership of thirty-one. The church building was once again destroyed by a storm in July 1942. Worship service was conducted in the school building until June 9, 1945. The first lot on First Avenue and Seventh Street was sold, and three lots were purchased on the corner of First Avenue South and Ninth Street. Plans were made for a new building, and the foundation was poured in June 1946.

The building was completed later that year and is now a Recognized Texas City Monument. Ground was broken on May 20, 1984, to add on an annex to the church; Reverend Kelley Black was assigned as the pastor. The annex was consecrated on July 14, 1985, under the pastorate of Reverend Perrie Joy Jackson, under her tenure, major renovation of the interior of the sanctuary was completed. The congregation held bake sales and yard sales to bring in revenue to the Church. Reverend Darnell Thomas was assigned as pastor from 1990-1994. Many items were made of wood and sold for the Annual Church Bazaar, giving monetary and manual support to all organizations.

Reverend J.D. Brown, 1994-1998, offered spiritual support to the homebound members of the church with visits and scripture readings through Bible lessons. Also, prayer services were faithfully held on Friday evenings.

Reverend Henry Fred Hynson, 1998-2005, was instrumental in reorganizing the youth for Lakeview Camp programs. He organized the Little Lambs Choir and Praise Dancers, instituted the Resurrection Revival and Youth Revival, which was held at the Texas City Dike. He was also instrumental in getting our apportionments paid in full. Reverend Hynson was instrumental in getting a Van to bring our children and adults to/from the church.

Reverend Carolyn E. Robinson became pastor in June 2005, as well as pastoring St. Paul in Galveston, Texas, until June 2009. During this time, two Hurricanes hit Galilee (Katrina and Rita), with damage to the roof and the interior of the entire church. We have had major reconstruction done to the fellowship hall, kitchen, classrooms, hallway, pastor's study, and the sanctuary. The parsonage has been completely remodeled, the van was paid off, and we no longer in debt to the I.R.S. Finally, under her helm, the church received a $20,000 Dunn grant to strengthen our Ministry with the youth in the area and enlighten them of special events available and new experiences around Galveston and Harris counties.

Reverend Keith J. Bell was assigned to pastor Galilee in June 2011, and he was a blessing for us. Galilee was blessed with plenty of new growth during his tenure. We give God all the glory for his leadership.

We restarted our Prayer Meetings, Bible Study, Sunday School, and our Senior Choir. Pastor Bell also founded 4 R.E.A.L. (Restoring, Empowering, Anointing Lives), a Young Adult-Ministry, and a Food Pantry.

Galilee U.M. Church was blessed with an Associate Pastor, Rev. Diedra J.A. Walters, the year of 2010 with gifts and graces and a strong desire to give herself away to further the building of His Kingdom and the healing of His people. In her ministry, she sowed seeds of love, hope, and peace, as well as nurtured God's people. Pastor Diedra served as the grant administrator for the Dunn Grant, Rock Solid: Through Christian Education, Cultural Awareness and Self-Development, which is designed to enrich and fund our youth programs.

Galilee United Methodist Church has a roster of 12 Pastors not mentioned in the History Write-up:

- Reverend Willie McGowen
- Reverend Williams
- Reverend White
- Reverend F.D. Lee
- Reverend Thigpen
- Reverend N.W. White
- Reverend S. Jones
- Reverend E.W. Akins
- Reverend Andrew Harris (served 17 yrs. As Senior Pastor at G.U.M.C.)
- Reverend D.W. Houston
- Reverend Collie Polk, Jr.
- Reverend M.D. Lamb

July 1, 2015.
"It's a New Season. It's a New Day!" Galilee United Methodist Church is very grateful to welcome the Reverend William Sowell as our new

Senior Pastor. The congregation looks forward to a bright and prosperous future during his tenure, if it will be God's will.

BIBLE
The Faces of Sou
DR. MARTIN LUTHER KING, JR.
(JANUARY 15, 1929 - APRIL 4, 1968)
SPECIAL THANKS
CITY OF TEXAS CITY GRATEFULLY ACKNOWLEDGES MARY ELLEN AND CHARLES "CHUCK" DOYLE FOR THEIR GENEROSITY IN PROVIDING THE FUNDING FOR THE DR. MARTIN LUTHER KING, JR. STATUE.

Reference

Barbour's Chapel Baptist Church. (n.d.). Church history, membership rolls, anniversary programs, and congregational oral traditions. (Internal archives).

City of Texas City. (n.d.). City history, planning documents, municipal archives, and historic zoning maps. Texas City, TX.

City of Texas City Planning Department. (n.d.). Zoning ordinances, land use maps, and redevelopment plans.

Galilee Methodist Church. (n.d.). Founding documents, membership records, ministry archives, and oral traditions. (Internal archives).

Galveston County Appraisal District. (n.d.). Historic parcel maps, property ownership records, and land use data. https://www.galvestoncad.org

Galveston County Historical Commission. (n.d.). Cemetery surveys, preservation records, and historical documentation.

Houston Chronicle. (n.d.). https://www.houstonchronicle.com

Interviews with descendants of the South Community. (various dates). Family oral histories documenting migration, church life, education, and the 1947 Texas City Disaster.

Larson, E. (2003). *City on fire: The explosion that devastated a Texas town*. Free Press.

Merrill, J. (1997). *The Texas City Disaster, 1947*. University of Texas Press.

Moore Memorial Public Library. (n.d.). Local history vertical files, oral histories, and newspaper archives. https://www.texascity-library.org

Moore Memorial Public Library Oral History Project. (n.d.). Community interviews and local memory archives.

National Archives. (n.d.). Texas City Disaster federal reports and Coast Guard investigations.

Newspapers.com. (n.d.). Texas City and Galveston County newspaper archives. https://www.newspapers.com

Roberts, A. (n.d.). Freedom Colonies research and scholarship. Texas A&M University.

Sanders/Vincent Community Center. (n.d.). Founding documents and program archives.

Texas City Independent School District. (n.d.). Booker T. Washington School records, building plans, and administrative documents.

Texas City Museum. (n.d.). Historical collections, photographs, community archives, and Texas City Disaster artifacts. https://www.texascitymuseum.org

Texas City Museum Oral History Collection. (n.d.). Recorded interviews with residents and disaster survivors.

Texas Freedom Colonies Project. (n.d.). *Texas Freedom Colonies Atlas*. https://www.thetexasfreedomcoloniesproject.com

Texas Historical Commission. (n.d.). *Cemetery Preservation Program & African American Cemetery Registry*. https://www.thc.texas.gov

Texas Historical Commission. (n.d.). *Texas Historic Sites Atlas*. https://atlas.thc.texas.gov

Texas State Historical Association. (n.d.). *African Americans*. In *Handbook of Texas Online*.

Texas State Historical Association. (n.d.). *Galveston County*. In *Handbook of Texas Online*.

Texas State Historical Association. (n.d.). *Great Depression in Texas*. In *Handbook of Texas Online*.

Texas State Historical Association. (n.d.). *Texas City*. In *Handbook of Texas Online*. https://www.tshaonline.org

The Galveston County Daily News. (n.d.). https://www.galvnews.com

Church Records & Programs

Barbour's Chapel Baptist Church. (1913–2005). *Church anniversary programs, membership rolls, and historical documents.* Texas City, TX.

Galilee Methodist Church. (1913–present). *Church records and historical archives.* Texas City, TX.

First Baptist Church of Texas City. (1905–present). *Church programs and historical documents.* Texas City, TX.

City & Institutional Records

Texas City Independent School District. (1937–1953). *Booker T. Washington School construction and administrative records.* Texas City, TX.

Texas City Government. (1952). *Annexation records for Virginia Point.* Texas City, TX.

Texas Historical Commission. (Various years). *Site files and historical markers for Texas City religious institutions.*

Historical Events

Texas City Disaster Relief Committee. (1947). *Reports and documentation of the Texas City Disaster.* Texas City, TX.

United States Army. (1913–1915). *Records of the First Provisional Aero Squadron and Second Division Encampment in Texas City.*

About the Author

Priscilla T Graham is a documentary historian, preservationist, and visual archivist whose work is dedicated to identifying, documenting, and safeguarding endangered Black communities and cultural landscapes across Texas and the American South. A Gulf War veteran and a fifth-generation descendant of Harriett Mitchell, her work is grounded in lineage, responsibility, and the ethical preservation of historical records.

Beginning in the mid-2010s, Priscilla conducted sustained field research in communities located within two hours of the Greater Houston Area, focusing on historic Black settlements shaped by emancipation, segregation, labor, and faith. In late 2014 and throughout 2015, this research brought her repeatedly to Texas City, where she encountered the South Community during a period when portions of its physical landscape were still intact. During that time, she photographed church buildings, streetscapes, and community spaces as part of a broader effort to document Black settlements before they disappeared.

In earlier research, including work related to the 1867 settlement, the South Community appeared only briefly, and the scale and speed of its physical erasure were not yet fully apparent. When Priscilla returned to Texas City in later years, the landscape had been completely altered. The churches and structures she had previously photographed no longer stood. Today, **Galilee Methodist Church is the only remaining church along First Avenue South**. Elsewhere, what remains consists of cornerstones, displaced artifacts, and commemorative materials preserved through institutional memory and the African American Cultural Park.

The photographs produced during those early visits became records of places that no longer exist. This experience fundamentally shaped the approach of *The Back Stories of History: Featuring South Community*. The work does not attempt to reconstruct the past through imagination or nostalgia. Instead, it preserves what was directly witnessed, documented, and later confirmed through archival sources, oral histories, and material artifacts. By presenting visual documentation alongside historical records and commemorative texts, the book ensures that the South Community is seen not only as it is remembered, but as it existed at the moment it was encountered.

For more than a decade, Priscilla has built one of Texas's most extensive contemporary archives of Black heritage, documenting settlements, churches, cemeteries, neighborhoods, and cultural institutions at risk of erasure. Her work integrates photography with archival research, oral history, and digitization, creating records that preserve cultural landscapes with accuracy, care, and respect.

Through her archival studio, **Harriett's History Box, LLC**, Priscilla continues to safeguard Black and Indigenous histories for future generations. Living and working in Arcola, Texas, she remains committed to documenting communities before they vanish and to preserving evidence of how they once lived, worshiped, and gathered—ensuring that what has been erased from the physical landscape remains present in the historical record.

www.ingramcontent.com/pod-product-compliance
Lightning Source LLC
LaVergne TN
LVHW020047110826
845155LV00029B/660

* 9 7 8 1 9 5 3 8 2 4 1 9 6 *